WHEN ONLY AN INDECENT DUKE WILL DO

ROMANCING THE RAKE

TAMMY ANDRESEN

Keep up with all the latest news, sales, freebies, and releases by joining my newsletter!

www.tammyandresen.com

Hugs!

Copyright © 2020 by Tammy Andresen

All rights reserved.

No part of this book may be reproduced in any form or by any electronic or mechanical means, including information storage and retrieval systems, without written permission from the author, except for the use of brief quotations in a book review.

❦ Created with Vellum

PROLOGUE

Early Spring London 1818

Raithe, the Baron of Balstead, watched as his last two victims walked through the door. Good. They were all here.

He'd carefully chosen this cast of characters, his soon-to-be house guests. He needed them for a very particular purpose, though he had no intention of telling them what that purpose was.

This was a situation where it was best to lie.

He found many situations were that way. Not all of them, of course. But here, at his gentlemen's club, where drinking and gambling were the primary activities, it was all about the bluff. Just to his right sat three friends. Lord Dashlane, Lord Crestwood and Lord Craven. They were his first three potential…guests.

Craven was one of the few men in England that actually frightened him a bit. Quiet and sullen, he was also tall and well-muscled. He looked quick as a snake and equally as deadly. Then there was Dashlane, Blond with a flashing smile, he was a charmer to be sure. Crestwood was dark-haired and handsome. All three liked their fair share of women and liquor but he'd seen them defend a group of harlots that another band of ruffians had attempted to rob and that put these gents on his list.

"Are you going to tell us what this is about?" Dashlane asked, bringing his whisky to his lips.

"In a minute," he answered, holding up a finger. A wide range of patrons/guests crowded the club tonight, seats limited, which worked for him. His last two players had entered the club but hadn't picked him out the crowd yet.

The Duke of Rathmore made his way through the mash of people and stopped directly in front of Raithe. Rathmore turned to his cousin and best friend, Lord Hartwell. "Don't you love the smell of leather, cigars, and good whisky?"

Hartwell rolled his eyes. "I prefer brandy and thank goodness we missed the speaker," he quietly announced as he brushed back his rich brown hair. "I've no appetite for politics today."

Rathmore raised his brow. "What's gotten into you?"

"Charlie." Hartwell grimaced, his mouth tightening.

Raithe's insides tightened. Charlie was short for Charlotte, Lady Charlotte Rainsville. She was Rathmore's cousin and Hartwell's sister. As vivacious as she was beautiful, she'd come out the season before. Fearless and outspoken, many had said she should have been born a man.

Not that her strong personality stopped her from garnering male attention. In fact, Charlie had been the premiere debutante last season with droves of men following her about but she'd yet to choose a husband. Raithe had not been one of those men. He stayed away from respectable girls as a general rule and Charlie in particular. Something about her beauty made her difficult to even look at. A man might lose his head and he couldn't afford to do that now.

"Are you worried for the upcoming season? I know you were beating men off with sticks and clubs." Rathmore chuckled.

Hartwell's grimace turned into a full-on spasm. "Worried doesn't begin to cover how I feel. And sticks and clubs were the least of the needed weapons. I had two incidents that involved a sword and one that required a pistol."

Chase clapped his cousin on the back. "I'll help you."

Hartwell gave him a light shove. "You said that last year too. But we both know you're too busy to help me keep Charlie out of trouble."

"Busy doing what?" Raithe asked, a light grin playing at his lips. He knew full well what sorts of illicit pastimes the duke engaged in that kept him occupied.

Both men turned to look at him. Hartwell appeared leery while Rathmore crossed his arms over his chest. "Don't sneak up on me like that."

"I didn't sneak." His grin broadened. "I've been sitting here the entire time. Isn't that right, Dashlane?"

"Are they who we're waiting for? Can we get on with it then?" Dashlane cracked his knuckles. "I've got a lovely brunette waiting for my attention."

Rathmore frowned at the other fellow. "Must you be so indiscrete about your indiscretions?"

Crestwood quirked a brow. "How else should a man be? We are young, single, titled. Seems perfect to me."

"It's tawdry. It's one thing to participate in such behavior but another to speak so openly about it."

Rathmore frowned and Raithe realized he should get this conversation moving before the men began to squabble. That could come later. "Gentlemen," he started, clearing his throat. "I'm having a party at the end of next week. You are the premier guests on the list."

Crestwood slapped the table, his attitude completely changing. "Now we're getting somewhere."

Craven continued to grimace; his face a complete mask. "What sort of party?"

"The sort men of your kind would like." He winked. Raithe had a particular sort of reputation for having parties filled with women and liquor. That wasn't what this was going to be and so he wouldn't outwardly promise such delights. It would give him plausible deniability later.

Rathmore dropped his arms to his sides. "Next week? I couldn't possibly."

Raithe tried not to frown. The duke, once a notorious rake, had hardly been seen at the gaming hells or at parties of ill repute. Coupled with his comments to Crestwood, that made him the most important candidate of them all.

Hartwell stepped forward. "We're headed to the coast to check in on some of our properties."

Excellent. He tightened his grip around his glass. "Then you'll be close to my home. Surely, you can spend a few days with us."

Hartwell shook his head. "My sister will be travelling with me. I seriously doubt she is suited to one of your parties."

Raithe didn't respond. This gathering would be perfectly appropriate for such a lady but he wasn't about to tell them all of that. Besides, Charlie was the last woman he wanted in his house, under his roof, near his bed. "That doesn't mean Rathmore can't attend. For a few days at least." He leaned forward. "Tell me you're not craving something different."

He saw the flicker of indecision in the other man's eyes.

Victory roared in his blood.

"Count me in," Crestwood crowed. "What about you, Dashlane?"

Dashlane took a sip of his drink. "Why not? I could use a change of pace. Craven?"

The third man frowned. "I suppose."

Raithe didn't care if Craven attended or not. In fact, he'd prefer he didn't but the three were often together making Craven a necessary evil. "Rathmore?"

"I'll think on it," Rathmore shrugged, staring at the far wall.

"I'll attend," another voice called from the corner. Raithe turned, his jaw clenching when he'd seen who spoke. His Grace, the Duke of Danesbury sat, partially obscured by shadow. The man was rarely seen out, his face having been scarred on one side from some accident or another. Raithe's eyes widened to see the man here on such a busy night. "Your Grace?" he asked. Strictly speaking the man was not invited but as a duke, he'd be difficult to refuse.

"I've heard of your parties, Balstead. I'll come if you'll have me."

Raithe swore softly under his breath. This was not one of the carefully chosen men. He didn't know what sort of man Danesbury was and didn't wish to find out. "Of course, Your Grace."

Raithe sat back in his chair. He had five men after all. Not the five he'd originally set out to invite but still… that ought to give Cassandra some choices…

CHAPTER ONE

Chase, better known as the Duke of Rathmore, stared out the window of his carriage, watching the darkening sky with a narrow-eyed glare. The clouds suited his mood. One might argue that he should be happy. He was on his way to a summer house party that was likely to be the event of the season.

At least for lords with power, money, and a proclivity for fun. And by fun, he meant drinking, gambling, and sex, likely in that order.

The Baron of Balstead, was known among most men to be a deviant. He liked lavish parties with high-powered men and lowly women. Chase had been invited before. But somehow, Balstead had managed to convince him to attend this time. As an unmarried duke who regularly showed up in the clubs, gaming hells, and even a few high-end brothels, he was exactly the sort that Balstead would want to attend. This was just the first time that Chase had ever accepted.

He wasn't sure why he'd decided to go this time. Perhaps it was the nagging feeling that had set in of late that something more meaningful was missing from his life. He'd become duke at the tender age of sixteen when his parents had died while crossing the English Channel during a storm. When he'd recovered from his grief, he'd set about enjoying all the benefits of being a young duke. But that had been ten years prior and the things he'd enjoyed had lost their shine.

And so, he'd decided the only answer was to search out even more ruckus fun in the form of Balstead's party. If he were honest, however, he wasn't certain the idea sat right in his mind. And so, he'd set out two days later than he'd planned. And he'd taken his time surveying several properties on the trip. And now, it looked as though he'd be delayed again as a fat plop of rain landed on the roof of his carriage.

Perhaps, he shouldn't go at all. The road he travelled followed along the coast, giving him scenic views of the ocean beyond. At least that's what some people would think of water. Right now, it was a dark, ominous grey that looked, to him, like a death trap.

He slapped his hand against his knee as more rain began to fall. He wasn't going forward or turning back tonight. Rapping on the carriage wall, he called to his driver. "Is there somewhere we can stop for the night?"

"Aye, Yer Grace," the driver called back. "We can keep travelling along this road and get to a little village called Seabridge Gate. It's quaint and quiet but it's our best bet for a night's reprieve from the storm."

"Sounds good," he called back, settling into his seat, the knot in his chest unfurling a bit. At least for today, the decision had been made not to go on. But that feeling of relief only lasted for a bit as the rain pummeled the carriage, the wind driving the water near sideways.

Another five minutes passed as Chase watched the ocean, the waves growing large and furious as they beat against the shore but soon the rain dulled even the view of the ocean's anger.

"Yer Grace," his driver hollered over the beating wind. "I see a home up ahead. Should we stop and seek shelter?"

He grimaced. The notion of asking a complete stranger for help filled him with dread. Who knew what he would find? "How much longer until we reach the village?"

"I don't rightly reckon," the driver answered. "But we're getting near soaked out here."

Chase sighed. "You're right. Let's stop." His valet and footman were also in attendance and while the footman was used to such conditions, his valet, Mr. Wendel, was not. Besides, no man should be out in a storm like this.

The carriage pulled up the drive, long and sweeping, rising up a hill. Not only would they be safe from the wrath of the ocean, they'd likely have excellent views. Soon, a stately manor house appeared and in moments, staff flooded out the doors to greet the unexpected guests.

Stepping down from the carriage, he followed a well-trained butler into a large entry. A portly but jovial fellow dressed in an immaculate evening coat swept down the stairs. "Welcome," he called as if Chase were an expected guest. "Welcome to Highland Manor. I am the Honorable Thomas Moorish. Whom do I have the honor of addressing?"

Chase gave a slight bow of his head, putting on his best dukely façade. "The Duke of Rathmore, at your service."

The man's eyes widened. "Your Grace," he breathed. "What brings you to my humble home?"

Chase's eyebrows lifted, giving the grand entry a sweep of his gaze. "Your home is lovely and the storm has stopped my travels, at least for the night. I wondered if I might be able to weather its wrath here and impose upon your fine hospitality."

The other man nodded. "We'd be most delighted to have such a guest."

Chase nodded again as he noted the *we* in the sentence. Did the man have a wife? Children? Then something wonderful caught his gaze. At the top of the stairs, one, two, three, four, five ladies appeared. Dressed in a rainbow of pastels, two brunettes, two blondes, and one redhead gazed down at him. At least that's how it appeared from his spot near the door. He couldn't quite make out any of them individually but the effect of all five was staggering. Had he wanted to keep driving? Damn fool. This was the perfect spot to weather a storm.

―――

Miss Ophelia Moorish stood at the top of the stairs and gazed down at the young duke. He was the stuff of fairy tales and romances and… She stopped, realizing she was getting carried away.

As a longtime lover of all books, she tended to cast herself as the heroine in the pages and make the people who surrounded her characters in her own story. It had gotten her in trouble on more than one occasion.

For example, last year she'd discovered a gelding that had gotten trapped in the sea grass that stretched for miles when the tide was out. She'd imagined herself the animal's great rescuer. Instead, it had nearly trampled her in its fear. She had gotten the horse safely out, but she'd suffered a broken arm from the experience.

Drawing a deep breath, she looked at the duke again. He'd removed his hat and dark hair waved back from his forehead and down over his ears. She couldn't see the color of his eyes, but his jaw was square and his shoulders broad. Her heart hammered in her chest again. He really was like a prince from a story.

And she could swear his gaze followed her every move. Was that her imagination again? She wasn't certain but her pulse accelerated even more.

"Girls," her father called from the bottom of the steps. "Come down and meet our guest."

One of her sisters, likely Bianca, giggled hysterically while Juliet fluttered her hand in the air. Ophelia pursed her lips. Apparently, she wasn't the only sister who had noticed the handsome duke.

As the eldest, however, she was most entitled to

seek his attention. She was nearly two and twenty and still had yet to participate in a proper season. Without a mother and with five sisters, her father hadn't been able to step away from his business and family in order to take her. Adrianna, her youngest sister, was about to turn eighteen. Her father threatened to unleash them all on London at once. Not conventional, but potentially necessary.

Ophelia sighed. She understood and she agreed. When their mother had passed, she'd taken up the role of mother figure with her young sisters and she didn't regret it a bit. But lately, she'd begun to wonder about her own future. Would there ever be time for her to find her own husband and have her own family? And what about the adventure of a season? The opportunity to live her own fairy tale before she settled into a future?

She had to confess, she loved children. Even when they cried or acted naughty. Caring for her sisters had been a blessing and she'd gladly do it again.

Her sisters stepped back, allowing her to make her way down the steps first. Gently, she lifted the front of her skirt, giving His Grace her best smile. He smiled back, and she nearly gasped with awe. He had the sort of flashing green eyes that made her heart race in her chest. His nose had a bit of a crook, but that only made him more masculine, while his mouth was full and completely…well…kissable. His shoulders were just as broad as she'd imagined and his skin-tight breeches left little question to the narrowness of his hips and muscles of his legs. His boots were polished to a high shine and she admired them for a moment before she realized she'd just given him a head to toe perusal.

Her gaze snapped back up to his eyes and he quirked one eyebrow as his smile broadened into a knowing grin. Heat flamed in her cheeks.

"Your Grace, this is my eldest daughter, Miss Ophelia Moorish."

She dipped into a deep curtsy, her cheeks still radiating heat as she murmured, "Your Grace."

Her father went down the line by age. "My second eldest, Juliet. Then we have Cordelia, Bianca, and lastly, Adrianna." Each woman curtseyed in turn but Ophelia noted that the duke's gaze returned to her the moment the introductions finished. Heat spread through her body at his sparkling emerald eyes.

"It's a pleasure, ladies." He subtly skimmed his gaze down her frame and Ophelia stared at the wall attempting not to blush again. She had a trim waist but she was fuller in her hips and bosom than most of her sisters. Then he looked to her father. "You sir have been blessed with a beautiful brood of daughters."

Her father chuckled. "I was handsome enough in my day and my wife, God rest her soul, was a beauty to be certain."

The duke's mouth tightened. "I'm sorry for your loss."

Her father waved his hand and the dull ache that always weighed Ophelia down at the mention of her mother, filled her limbs. She knew her father still hurt as well but he gave a small smile.

"Thank you kindly. Loss is never easy but today we have a reason to celebrate. Rarely do we have such a distinguished guest." Then he turned to his daughters. "What shall we do to turn this storm into a night of merriment?"

Ophelia, stepped forward, giving another small curtsy. "Perhaps we should ask His Grace."

As she came back up, their eyes met again and her breath stuttered in her throat.

"Dinner would be lovely," he answered, his deep baritone sending a thrill down her spine and making her stomach flutter.

"We could play music for you," Cordelia quietly volunteered. Though shy, she spoke best with an instrument and her pianoforte skills were beyond compare.

The duke gave a nod as Juliet clapped her hands. "And we could dance."

Bianca nodded enthusiastically. "Oh, that would be fun." Then she turned to the butler. "Would you tell the kitchen we have a guest? And have the music room ready."

But Ophelia turned to the duke. "Does that suit you, Your Grace?"

The intensity of his green eyes made her cheeks heat again. She truly felt like a princess being discovered by her prince the way he stared at her. Her favorite tale was *Cinderseat* and she imagined that this was just how Ella felt.

"It sounds lovely," he said. "I am very much looking forward to this evening."

So was she. Excitement sizzled along her skin when she thought about dancing with this magnificent man. Tonight felt like the party she'd wanted to attend for so long but hadn't had the opportunity. Finally, she had a chance to meet her prince.

CHAPTER TWO

Devilish ideas were swirling about his head as Chase assessed the eldest daughter of the Moorish clan. She had luxurious dark hair and sparkling brown eyes, which were set in a lovely porcelain and pink skin. High cheekbones, a pert little nose, and that mouth... Damn, he could spend a week devouring just her lips. His quick and subtle perusal of the rest of her told him that he'd need a great deal longer than just a week. She had the sort of figure that drove a man wild. Tiny in the middle with all sorts of curves. They made a man want to do bad things.

But he'd met beautiful women before. Hell, they practically tossed themselves in front of him at every opportunity. There was something different about this one. She was a bit older, not a girl in her first season, but still, she held an air of innocence. Or perhaps it was just optimism or kindness. Like her father. The pair of them oozed the sort of gentility and grace that his class was supposed to personify but so often did not. And they made him feel as though he were being wrapped in a warm blanket after years in a cold harsh world.

Which was why he'd leave the woman alone despite his obvious lust. How could he be the man to tarnish such a pure spirit? Then again, her lips called a siren song that left him weak and unable to think logically.

He squinted his eyes. Somehow referencing Odysseus made him think of other famous authors and the women's names made him pause. "Ophelia, Cordelia, Juliet?" He softly repeated. "Are they all…"

Mr. Moorish chuckled. "Guilty. I named them from various Shakespeare works. I'm an avid reader and a bit of a romantic."

A few of the ladies giggled while one of them rolled her eyes. He sincerely couldn't remember which sister she was. They were all lovely, to be certain, but Ophelia had captured his attention. He gazed at her again, hardly able to look at anyone else when one of the sisters spoke.

"Ophelia is exactly like him," her sister said. "Always has her nose in a book."

The words gave him the perfect excuse to drink in Ophelia's visage again. He wasn't at all surprised to know that she had more in common with her father. For a brief second, he wondered what it might be like to be around someone like Ophelia all the time. Would it grow tiring? Or would his worn view of the world shift?

He swiped those thoughts away. He'd stay here for tonight and tomorrow, when the storm had passed, he'd leave again and return to his life. Or the party. He still wasn't certain and he honestly didn't want to think about it right now.

"Just out of curiosity, how far is the village from here?" He wondered how close he was to passing this little slice of paradise.

"Seabridge Gate is just a few miles. We walk there in the nice weather." Mr. Moorish gestured to a room on their right. "Shall we sit and have a few refreshments?"

Chase stepped into the room. "Thank you. Is it a large village?"

"No," Ophelia answered, her honey voice washing over him. "Quite small. Not many take this coastal route so it's more the people who make it home."

He nodded as they all sat. "Is there an inn? We almost travelled there instead of stopping here." Not that it mattered now. His staff were surely huddled about the kitchen stove already.

"Yes, there is but again, it only has a few rooms. And even with the small number of travelers, it's likely to be full on a night like tonight." He pointed toward the window to the front of the house.

Rain soaked the panes making it difficult to see, but beyond that, a heavy downpour pummeled the ground and the ocean's waves crashed into the rocks. Normally he hated looking at the ocean in a storm, but he was safe enough here in this house sitting up high above the beach. "Whoever built this house was smart to set it up on this hill."

"It was our great grandfather, The Earl of Seabridge," one of the women answered. "Made from heavy stone, it was meant to withstand cannon fire, wind, water, basically anything England or its invaders could throw at it."

"Quite right, Cordelia," Mr. Moorish said. "My grandfather was very smart in his holdings and made sure to provide for all his children and grandchildren after them."

A younger, very pretty blonde spoke up next. "And you'll do the same for us, right Papa?"

"That I will, Adrianna." He reached for his daughter's hand just as a tray of snacks was carried in by a footman. "Now, let's allow our guest to eat."

Ophelia rose and began pouring steaming cups of tea. "How do you like yours, Your Grace?"

His women or his tea? He supposed the answer was the same. Steaming hot and very sweet, he thought to himself and then clenched his teeth together. "Milk and one lump of sugar, please."

Ophelia did as he requested and then carefully handed him the delicate china. His hands were large but he'd a lifetime of practice balancing delicate cups in his long fingers. Still, he inadvertently brushed hers as he took the cup.

Every muscle in his body tensed with a longing he hadn't thought possible. She leaned over slightly, smiling down at him and he wanted to pull her into his lap and worship that mouth. Maybe he needed to attend that party after all, considering how he lusted after an innocent woman right now.

OPHELIA HELD her breath as the final notes of Cordelia's piece on the pianoforte echoed about the room. The haunting song had been magnificent and suited to the weather outside. She clapped with pride as Cordelia finished.

"That was just marvelous," she gushed, looking

over at the duke who sat next to her on the settee. "Don't you think?"

They'd passed the evening pleasantly with a lovely meal and had retired to the music room afterward.

"I think a sister who supports her sibling so enthusiastically is quite marvelous too."

She pressed her hands to her cheeks, looking at the floor. He'd peppered her with compliments like that all evening. He'd given a few to her sisters too, of course. But her entire family had noticed the attention he'd paid her and they stared at the two of them now. "Do you have any siblings, Your Grace?"

"No," he answered, sitting back a bit. "I had a brother but he died when I was very young."

She frowned, wishing she could touch him in support. Something in the tension in those broad shoulders, the angle of his chin told her that he hurt from the loss. "I'm so sorry. My sisters are my world. I can't imagine not having them." She meant every word. Turning toward him, she very lightly brushed her hand against his as Cordelia began another song. "Do you have other family?"

He shook his head and subtly grasped her fingers, hiding the touch behind her skirts. "I do have one rather annoying cousin who pesters me often. The

Marquess of Hartwell. He also has a younger sister whom I adore."

"Pesters you?" She raised her eyebrows, trying to keep up with the conversation though she was completely distracted by his touch. It was exactly as she'd pictured romance to begin.

He gave a tiny wink. "All right. You've caught me. He keeps me sane and grounded most times. Though, he did caution me against this leg of the trip."

"Why is that?" Ophelia leaned closer, her shoulder just brushing his. Nervous flutters erupted over her skin. This sort of flirting was exactly what she'd always hoped for and she tried to etch every touch into her memory.

She felt his muscles tense against hers. "I'm to attend a house party but the guests aren't the most savory members of society. Lord Hartwell and Lady Charlotte stopped just south of here, but I continued on to join the merriment."

That made her lean back to look at him, study the tight lines in his face. "Unsavory company near here?" The village, her father often jested, was the most wholesome spot in all of England. Everyone knew everyone, people were kind and nurturing. Of course, she'd known every man here for most of her life, which had made finding a husband rather difficult, but overall it was a lovely place to live.

The duke lifted a shoulder, looking down at his lap. "A day's ride. Closer to Ipswich."

"Ah," she nodded. "Were you summering by the sea?"

He shook his head. "I came from London."

Passing through here to get to Ipswich? "I don't quite understand how you arrived here. This is the rather long way to reach your destination."

He glanced up at her again. "I suppose it is. I was using the journey as a bit of time to think…" His fingers squeezed hers. "Away from all the pressures in the city." He winked then. "And my cousin has a property just south of Seabridge Gate. It's his favorite so we're there often."

She wanted to ask him more. Her lips parted but she closed them again. Cordelia's second piece was drawing to a close and she didn't dare ask him more. She wasn't certain probing for more information was her place and she didn't want anyone else to overhear their conversation.

Cordelia immediately launched into an upbeat folk song and His Grace stood, momentarily letting go of her hand but then reaching it out to her again. "Would you care to dance?"

She looked to her father who gave her a wink. "No objection from me."

She turned back to Lord Rathmore. "I'd be honored." This time, as she slipped her fingers into his, her entire family watched. He led her to the middle of the open floor and suddenly, his hand was on her waist, her fingers clasped in his much larger ones. Heat radiated from his body and the subtle scent of sandalwood and a deeper male musk assaulted her senses. How had she never noticed how good a man smelled. Or was that just him?

Then he started the steps of a fun country dance and she didn't think about his seductive masculine aroma anymore instead, caught up in the feel of him as they moved together. Dancing with a handsome Duke, being swept away by him, had filled her daydreams and night fantasies since she'd come of age…maybe even earlier.

CHAPTER THREE

DAMN THIS WOMAN FELT GOOD. And she'd looked at Chase with such understanding, her face soft, her eyes warm and crinkled at the corners. Hell, he'd wanted to confess his darkest secrets to her. Which was ridiculous. He'd done that with a woman once at the tender age of eighteen. His parents were gone and he'd been lonely. She was the daughter of a baron and he'd thought he might marry her. Only she told half of London about his confessions, his secret pain.

It had taken years for people to stop calling him the forlorn duke afterward. Of course, nowadays they more often referred to him as the indecent duke, but that he could live with. He'd earned that title after years of debaucherous behavior. Sometimes he wondered if behaving badly was all he was good at.

He gave her waist a small squeeze, wishing that he could pull her close. She had a slightly sweet scent like strawberries warmed in the summer sun and he wondered how she'd taste.

The song ended all too soon and he was obligated to dance with her other sisters. Normally, he would have appreciated each one of them for their attributes but he couldn't see anyone but Ophelia tonight. She'd entranced him with her beauty and charm. As the evening grew later, he'd wondered how he'd ever sleep. Between the weather and the storm Ophelia was creating in his head, he'd be up all night at this rate.

"Tell me." He leaned over toward Ophelia, a bit of a plan hatching in his brain. "You said that you and your father are avid readers. Is there a library in your fine home? I fancy some reading before bed."

"We do." She gave him that wide, lovely smile that spoke of unreserved joy. Then she turned to her father. "Papa, His Grace would like to see the library. May I take him?"

Her father nodded. "Excellent idea. Bring Adrianna with you."

Adrianna? Which one was she? He was having a

difficult time keeping track of all the women but the shortest sister, a waifish blonde, rose from a chair.

She rolled her eyes. "Papa, you know I don't like the library. Why can't Juliet go?"

"Hush," her father softly chastised. "Keep them company." Then he brushed his hands through the air, shooing them out the door.

Adrianna trailed behind as Ophelia linked her hand in his arm. He heard Adrianna mutter something about the most boring duke ever and he pressed his lips together to keep from laughing. Ophelia led them into the library, and even he stopped in awe. The cavernous room rose two stories with a balcony all along with second level and two spiral staircases to reach the upper books. "I'm impressed."

Ophelia tugged on his arm. "We've impressed a duke? That is something."

His eyes strayed to her again. He was interested in more than the library. Adrianna plopped down in a chair and leaned back, closing her eyes. "Tell me when you're done. I'm going to nap while I wait."

He clenched his teeth together, a wolfish grin threatening to give away the game. Had Mr. Moorish known that his other daughter would be a lenient chaperone? How interesting. And while

Ophelia was surely an innocent, he couldn't help but want to touch her. Just a little.

"What would you like to read?" Ophelia asked, leading him toward the spiral stairs.

"I'm not certain," he answered, sure he would make this meeting last as long as possible. "What are my options?"

"Let's begin with fiction or nonfiction," she said, stopping once again.

"For tonight, fiction. Something I can lose myself in and not think of what's happening around me."

She cocked her head to the side, studying him for a moment. "Excellent choice. Let's go up the stairs to where the romance and mysteries are located." Then she slipped her hand from his arm and started up one of the spiral stairs. He followed her keenly aware of the sway of her hips. Hellfire, the woman was built for sin. He wanted to reach out and grab that tiny waist again, pull her close to his body and feel his—

"Decision time," she said, looking back at him over her shoulder. "Mysteries are to the left, romances to the right."

He squeezed his eyes shut, the vision of her looking over her shoulder at him more than he could bare. Desire raged through his body, making his breeches uncomfortably tight. "Romance."

She gave a little gasp. "That's my favorite too."

"Which Shakespeare work is Ophelia in? Remind me." He knew, of course.

"Hamlet," she said, stopping. "But that's not a romance, it's a tragedy. I've asked my father why he'd name me after such a sad character, but he's convinced I'll learn from her mistakes. Isn't that odd?"

"Perhaps," he said, paying it only half a mind. The much larger part of his brain was focused solely on the curve of her rear and the way her loose coif cascaded down her back.

"We're back to what you might like to read." She stopped and turned toward him.

Desire made his fist clench and he pressed the closed hand against his thigh. Had he been admiring her backside? One look at her porcelain skin and lips the color of the inside of a seashell and he never wanted to look at anything else ever again.

"What's your favorite?" he asked. He didn't care what book they left with. He just wanted this stolen time alone with her. She set down the candle she held and ran her finger along the spine of several books. He watched its delicate brush picturing those same fingers trailing down his bare chest.

"So many, it's hard to choose. I like fairy tales." She gave a long, sweet sigh that ruffled the nerves along his skin. "*Cinderseat*, for example. When the prince saves her from her wretched life." She turned back to him. "It's so wonderful."

"I'll read that one then," he said quietly, but he dropped his voice low and deep as he stepped closer.

She pulled the book from the shelf, then handed it to him. As he took it, their fingers brushed again but this time he tightened his grip. They were in the dark, quiet second story of the library. And he ached for this woman the way he hadn't wanted anything or anyone in ages.

What was the harm in one small kiss?

He argued that to a country woman like herself it might really mean something. But then again, she loved romance and perhaps, she wanted this stolen kiss as much as he did? Pulling her closer, he reached his other hand up to touch the velvety softness of her cheek. He skimmed his thumb over the lovely plump skin of her lower lip even as her warm breath blew across the sensitive fingertip.

Fitting her body against his, he lowered his head, reveling in the feel of her supple curves pressed against his hard angles. He couldn't wait to find out how she'd taste.

In all her wildest imaginings, and she'd had many, Ophelia had never pictured such a perfect scenario for a first kiss. First, this wasn't a boy from the village, or even a man from one of the local manors, but a handsome duke who'd landed on her doorstep during a storm. In addition, she and His Grace were in her favorite place in all the world, the library. Together, they were holding her most cherished story in their joined hands. His body pressed to hers and, in all her wondrous daydreams, she'd had no idea the male body would feel so…so…masculine. So hard, strong, warm to the point of near hot, and thrumming with an energy that made her pulse race.

Soft candlelight flickered about them as his warm breath, with the faintest scent of brandy and cigar, caressed her cheeks. This moment was so perfect, her hands shook with excitement as his lips descended toward hers.

Her breath came in short gasps and her heart pounded in her chest. This perfect moment was going to culminate in the most beautiful kiss. His lips touched hers, warm and firm, but oh so tender. The way his mouth moved over hers felt better than anything she'd dreamed. She held his biceps, her fingers digging into the bulging muscles to steady herself. Tingles raced through her body as he lifted his lips and then pressed them to hers again and again while sliding his hand down her neck and over her collarbone. Ophelia shivered at the light touch, goose pimples raising on her flesh. The moment was beautiful, exciting, intoxicating and she never wanted it to end.

He skimmed his fingertips over her chest, then they slid down her breast and across her nipple. The skin puckered at the touch and delightful sensations spread out from her mounded flesh but she drew back a bit, looking up into his face. His eyes were dark with his stare intent. He was even more handsome this close and yet the interaction had lost the rosy glow that had ringed the kiss moments before.

In every book she'd ever read, with every romantic kiss the hero had not slid his hand to the woman's nipple. This wasn't quite right.

Her mind was jelly, her knees nearly as bad, but a warning bell she couldn't quite articulate sounded in her head. Gently, she pressed against his chest to push him back.

He slid his palm back to her shoulder and lifted his head. "That was nice," he murmured, taking the book from her hand. "Thank you."

Thank you? Her gaze narrowed as she looked up at him. Those might be the very last words she wanted to hear. *Thank you?* "You're welcome?"

He gave her a relieved smile. "I shall enjoy the

book tonight, I'm sure." Then deliberately, he spread his fingers out on the small of her back and began leading her toward the spiral stairs. "What a delightful evening this has been."

Perhaps it was the fact that she'd had a moment to recover from that kiss, but her mind snapped into focus. He hadn't uttered the words *I love you* or even *I want to marry you* and certainly not *I'd like to see you again*. Had she kissed incorrectly? It was her first time. But she'd enjoyed the touch so much. Was it possible he hadn't?

Surely, as a duke, he knew that a man did not go around kissing his host's daughters unless he seriously considered marriage. But then again, he'd caressed her in a highly inappropriate way. Perhaps dukes had a different set of rules from other men? "I'm curious to know, Your Grace…" She stopped midway down the steps, keeping him from continuing down the stairs as she blocked the path. "What your plans are for tomorrow?"

He hesitated, standing on the stair above her. He towered over her but she kept her spine straight as she tilted her chin to look up at him. "I plan to continue on my journey as soon as the weather allows."

She gasped in a sharp breath. This was exactly like the other times she'd allowed her imagination to get carried away. She'd pictured him the hero, her prince, and herself as the heroine ready for a romantic adventure. But that wasn't what had just happened at all. She'd been just a rainy night's distraction for him. Her heart, which had been slowly sinking back down to Earth, crashed on the floor.

CHAPTER FOUR

Chase sat in his room reading the fairy tale that Ophelia had recommended. It had to be well past midnight but tired as he was, he couldn't sleep. The storm raged outside, battering the house with wind and rain as the ocean created a cacophony of waves. He hated the sound of an angry ocean. Memories plagued him now of his parents setting off for France. It was a short trip and he'd stayed home, due back at Oxford, but they'd promised to visit him at school once they'd returned.

Of course, he'd had three weeks before he'd had to be back. School had been an excuse to avoid the trip.

He never saw his parents again. A storm had risen in the channel passing, taking down their smaller vessel. He'd imagined a thousand times what their final moments must have been like and with each imagining, he hated the ocean a bit more. His chest was so tight, he clasped his hand over his heart. Why had he come this way at all?

But he knew. He'd set out to this party searching for something and somehow, he sensed the ocean held the answer.

Scrubbing his face, he looked down at the book in his hand. Here was a pure woman being abused by her stepmother. He could see the appeal and clearly both Mr. Moorish and his daughter had a penchant for stories. No wonder Ophelia liked this one. In the end the prince saved the girl. His mouth twisted. Had she pictured him to be her prince? What would she need to be saved from? Certainly not an abusive parent.

But still, she'd spent the rest of the evening, glaring at him as though he'd betrayed her. He likely had. He gave an audible sigh that the wind drowned out. He'd known he shouldn't kiss a woman like her. She was too innocent, but Chase had gotten caught up in the moment too, which wasn't like him at all. She was so beautiful, both in looks and personality, he'd wanted to steal just a small taste of that for himself. The problem was, despite how he'd dismissed her after the kiss, one taste hadn't been nearly enough.

He scrubbed his face. A better man would just marry her after what he'd done. She was an earl's granddaughter after all. And he doubted he'd get tired of bedding her. But then again, he was the sort of man who attended orgies, who bedded scores of women, who gambled and drank to his heart's content. Who buried his grief over the loss of his parents in scores of meaningless sexual trysts. And Ophelia…well she was near perfect. That disappointment he'd seen in her eyes tonight after their kiss, it made him cringe to remember. Not that there was an alternative. Were he to succumb to guilt and marry a woman like her, he'd have to get used to such glances, he was bound to disappoint her.

It hadn't always been this way. He stood, pacing the floor for about the tenth time since he'd come upstairs. He loved his parents but the world without them had been such a hard, cruel place. Yes, he had every material thing he needed to live in luxury, but his grief, the pain of losing them, had made his heart harder too. He stood at the window, tapping his foot as he stared out into the rain-soaked black night. He didn't know if that boy was still inside him, the one who'd loved and been loved in return. Was that what was missing?

A soft knock at the door pulled him from his thoughts. "Who is it?"

"Ophelia," a soft high voice called back.

Desire, relief, and anticipation pulsed through him as he quickly crossed the room and opened the door. She stood on the other side, her hair in a loose plait dangling over one shoulder while several tendrils floated about her face. Her cheeks held that same rosy glow, her body wrapped in a dressing gown as she crossed her arms over her chest. "I'm glad you're here," he said before he could hold it back. Gone was the thin veneer of calm he'd held up between them after the kiss. All the memories that had flooded him had made him raw inside.

She wrinkled her nose. "And why is that?"

He stopped, noting the jaunty angle of her jaw, the downturn of her mouth. She wasn't here to share another kiss, that was for certain. Disappointment settled heavily in his stomach. He'd likely never admit this to anyone, but that kiss had been the best in his life. She'd fit against him the way no other woman ever had and, for a moment, he'd lost his senses and nearly confessed being in love. Which was ridiculous. He was a seasoned rake, a duke, and a debaucher of the first order. He didn't fall in love after a single kiss. "I like the book you lent me."

She dropped her hands and her brows raised. "Really? Is the story what's causing you to pace so excessively? Every time I fall asleep, you start up again."

His lips parted in surprise. "You can hear me?"

"Your room is above mine," she answered, crossing her arms again. "I beg you, if you're going to continue your night wandering, do so in the library." She tapped her foot. "You've already stolen my first kiss, you need not also rob me of an entire night's sleep."

Those words hit him like a blow to the chest. That was her first kiss? Bloody hell, what would her second kiss be like? Her third? Damn, he had the distinct urge to pull her against him and find out. "My apologies for keeping you awake and for kissing you. I did not intend to steal anything. I—" He reached for her but she jerked away.

"Kindly do not touch me, Your Grace. Letting you do so is a mistake I will not make again."

He lowered his hand, his insides twisting in regret. "You don't think it will be a nice memory for both of us? That kiss we shared?" It would be for him. But then again, he wasn't worth much as far as he could tell.

Her nose lifted higher into the air. "When my real Prince Charming arrives, you will be the devil he helps me overcome. He'll be honorable and kind and surely teach me how it feels to be kissed by a man who truly values me."

He pulled back his chin, digging his fingers into his thigh. Her words hurt more than he cared to admit, not that he didn't deserve them. But she deserved to know the truth.

A SURGE of victory sang in her veins. Not every woman got the opportunity to tell the man who'd wronged her what a devil he was. She shot him another glare, sure that he'd be crestfallen from such a good put down.

Instead, he leaned casually against the frame of the door. She'd already noted that his jacket and cravat had been removed, and his shirt was undone at the neck, revealing a good bit of muscle and dark hair. The sort, she could confess, she'd like to run her fingers through. She curled her offending digits into her housecoat. She'd not touch this man ever again.

"That's the thing that can be difficult to explain," he said, his voice dropping lower in pitch so that his deep baritone absolutely vibrated through her. "Somehow the stolen kisses, the ones you shouldn't have, are that much sweeter." Then he pushed off the frame of the door and took a step closer. He didn't touch her but he stood within an inch of her much smaller frame. His heat seeped through her clothes and she remembered the hard press of his body. She'd wager, not that she ever did, that he'd feel even better with less clothing between them.

"If you come any closer to me, I'll scream." Her breath hitched but it wasn't because she was afraid. She likely should be. She was alone with a man who could ruin her or worse but somehow, she didn't believe he'd actually hurt her. Instead, her pulse raced with excitement. Deep inside, she knew his words were the truth. He wasn't quite her Prince Charming the way she'd first thought. There was something darker and a bit more dangerous behind his handsome charm and frankly, that bit of devil inside him was…exciting.

"There's no need for screaming. I promise you I'll never hurt you. Our kiss, though I am to blame, was given willingly from both parties." He licked his lips. Not overtly, more like a nervous gesture someone did when thinking. It still made her insides pulse with desire. "All I want to say is that if you ever desire another secret kiss, one that steals your breath and curls your toes. then you find me. I'll give you as much or as little as you wish, but give it to you I shall."

She hadn't realized she'd been backing up until she hit the wall behind her. Casually, he raised a hand and placed it on the plaster next to her head. Then he leaned toward her. She didn't want him to kiss her again, she told herself. She was in search of a prince or a knight in shining armor who lifted her up out of her ordinary life and swept her into her own fairy tale of adventure and romance that settled into a binding union. One where they married and had a family but also loved each other fiercely and, in that love, had their own secret adventure. This man was no knight, she'd already learned that. The problem was, he was making her insides molten fire, burning with desire. Her chest rose and fell as he leaned close enough to nearly kiss her. "Do not touch me," she managed to say through ragged breaths.

He frowned, one corner of his mouth drawing down. "Ophelia, I won't do anything you don't want me to." He pulled back a bit. "I'm simply telling you that you can trust me to obey any limits that you set forth. I liked your kiss more than I ever imagined and I'd very much like to kiss you again." His jaw tightened a muscle twitching in his cheek. "I'm not the man to give you more but I wish—"

She lifted her eyebrows. If she were honest, she found his predatory stance rather intoxicating but that was because it was dangerous. "Back up," she said, drawing in a long breath to steady her nerves.

He did, instantly. The ache between her legs pulsed again. Even more intoxicating than his dominant behavior was his obedience. She tried to calm her racing pulse. This was no fairy tale. What throbbed between them now was real and sharp and full of peril.

"I wish I could be the man you wanted. Good and light. A hero to carry you away…"

Ophelia gasped. How did he know what kind of man she wanted? "I never said—"

"Of course you didn't." He reached across the gap between them, brushing back a single lock of her hair. It slipped through his fingers. "I still know that's what you want just as I understand I'm not the man to give it to you. That man died a long time ago." He grimaced. "I can only give you what you see now. It isn't much, I know, but it's yours if you want it."

Her brows drew together as her hand settled over her thrumming heart. Did she? In this moment, it was so difficult to tell.

CHAPTER FIVE

EVERY MUSCLE in Chase's body coiled in an anticipation, ready to spring. The kiss in the library had been satisfying in ways he couldn't describe. It had been a soothing balm to his wounded soul. But this moment was like pouring hot coals onto a burning fire. She looked up at him, her mouth softly parted, her wide brown eyes crinkled with indecision, her chest heaving. Part of him knew that if he pushed, she'd consent. Allow him to taste her sweet strawberry nectar again.

But another part didn't want to. Yes, he desired her, more so than he had any woman for a long time. And certainly he'd meant his offer. But he also wished she didn't take it. He'd remember her as the one pure thing he'd touched in so long. If he sullied that now, what would he be left with, really? No wonder he hated himself. He was baiting the one good thing he'd touched in a long time to turn bad.

"So you can only give me a few stolen, secret kisses? That's it?" Her gaze had narrowed, her lips pressed into a firm line.

Good girl, he thought. He wanted to kiss her even more but he eased back a bit. "That's right."

"Bah," she said, slicing her hand through the air. "Are you married?"

"No," he returned, his fingers itching to touch her hair again. It had been so silky against the tips of his fingers.

"Deformed?" One eyebrow lifted as she stepped toward him.

He liked that comment less. "Of course not." He clenched his fists again, fighting the urge to pull her close. To kiss her lips.

"Then you're lying. You are capable of offering me far more." She reached out and pushed him square in the chest. Not hard, but enough to express her irritation. But her hand stayed pressed against him with nothing but his shirt between them. "One might argue, you are honor-bound to do so unless you are physically unable." Triumph shone in her eyes as she stopped moving forward and instead straightened her spine. "Men have married for far less than we've done tonight."

He let out a rumbling sound that must have vibrated through her hand because she snatched it away. "You don't know what you ask."

"I didn't ask anything." Then she shook her head. "Never mind. I can assure you, Your Grace, that I will never seek you out for another kiss. I came up here to ask you to be quieter and now I will say my farewell to you in hopes that it is forever."

Then she turned and started down the hall. He hated watching her walk away. It bothered him far more than he cared to admit. But she was right. It was likely best they sever their relationship now. Still, the pit of his stomach grew heavy with regret. "I'd prefer we leave each other on better terms."

She spun back around to him, her hands clenched in fists at her sides. "I won't tell my father about our kiss, but I expect you to continue on your way first thing tomorrow morning."

He grimaced, turning toward his room. He should have just kissed her. Or never kissed her. Chase couldn't be certain but he stopped at the threshold. "Ophelia," he called and she paused, looking back over her shoulder. "My given name is Chase. When you think of me, I'd like you to know my name. The name my parents used for me."

The sadness in his voice and in the words nearly knocked her breath from her lungs. She noted the past tense of his statement first. His parents no longer used that name or his parents were gone? "Used?" she whispered, her feet pivoting back around. "What do they use now?"

She watched as his brows drew together, his face tightening in pain, his mouth pinching. "They died a long time ago. I've been the duke since I was sixteen."

She gasped, then covered her mouth with her hands to hide her reaction. She remembered the pain of losing her mother. But she'd had her father and all her sisters from which to draw comfort. He'd told her he only had a single cousin. Who had helped him through the grief? She took two steps toward him, holding out her hand. Belatedly she realized her fingers trembled a bit. "What that must have been like for you. I can't imagine. You poor—"

"Ophelia," he said, his voice holding a note of desperation. "Don't paint me to be the victim here in need of saving."

She snapped her mouth shut. How had he figured her out so quickly? "I lost my mother. I know how it hurts."

He drew in a long breath. "I didn't tell you about my parents so that you would come back in my arms and kiss me out of sympathy. If you do kiss me again, it will be for lust."

Those words made her stop. Clearly, she'd allowed her romantic musings to carry her away once again. "I'm sorry for your loss."

Then, before anything else could be said, she fled, her feet flying across the thick carpet all the way to the stairs and then down them to her room. But after she'd returned to the safety of her bed chamber, she could still hear him above her. First walking and then tossing and turning in his bed.

And worse still, his words echoed in her thoughts. He'd lost his parents, suffered alone, well that thought was hers. But still, she could hear the sadness beneath his words. And somehow, despite being extremely handsome and a duke, no less, he didn't really value himself. She rolled over in bed, wondering if there was something she could do.

Finally, after what felt like hours, Ophelia decided that she needed to talk with him again. If she could control her attraction to him long enough to really listen, perhaps she could help him overcome his past and see his own value. He might not be the most moral man she'd ever met but he was redeemable. She could see real good in him. Finally deciding on a course of action, she fell asleep, just as the sky began to lighten.

She woke a few hours later to full sun pouring into her windows. What time was it? Hurrying out of bed, she fumbled about her room, attempting to wash her face and tame her hair. Sleep still weighed heavily on her mind but her maid was able to help her get ready and down to the breakfast room.

Just outside the door, she noted the sounds of her family talking, a good sign she wasn't too late. But the moment she walked through the doorway, silence fell and every eye turned to her. She noted that while all her sisters were there, her father wasn't present.

Sharp dread tightened her chest as they stared at her. She stopped, looking at several of them before she finally relaxed enough to ask. "What's wrong?"

Cordelia cleared her throat. "He left."

"Papa?" she asked, sliding into her seat near the head of the table. "He often starts work early in order to have the evenings with us."

"We're aware of our own father's schedule," Juliet huffed. "The subject we are less educated on is what happened between you and the duke that he left before seven this morning."

Ophelia nibbled her lip, trying to decide what she shared and didn't with her sisters. She loved her family dearly but there were very few secrets in this house. "Nothing happened. I—"

"Liar," Adrianna pointed across the table. "You kissed him last night. I know you did."

Heat infused her cheeks. "Adrianna, that's absurd. I—"

She turned her finger up and wagged it. "Don't deny it. It was completely obvious."

Her other sisters fell silent as they stared at her. Not knowing what to say, she gazed down at her hands currently twisting in her lap.

"Are you going to marry him?" Bianca finally asked.

Her head snapped up as she started in surprise. "He's gone. How could I marry him?"

"But…" This from Cordelia again. "He's coming back." She reached for one of her dark larks of hair and twisted it around her finger. "I thought perhaps he'd gone to get a marriage license."

"Coming back," she repeated, more to herself as she slumped down into her chair. Why would he be coming back? "He won't be bringing a marriage license. He made it clear he didn't want to marry. I've no idea why he would return."

"But that makes no sense," Bianca pinched her chin. "Father looked so happy the duke would be returning. One of you must be mistaken."

Ophelia's shoulders hunched. "It's Papa. But still, I'm glad he'll return. Even if he doesn't want to marry me, he did divulge some of his past and the man needs help."

Juliet groaned, loudly, drowning out any other noise in the room. "For heaven's sake, Ophelia. Please tell me you're not going to try and rescue a man who has made it clear he doesn't want you."

Ophelia straightened, bristling. "What does him wanting me have to do with helping him? We don't help people to get something out of it. We do it out of the kindness of our hearts."

Cordelia reached for her sister's hand. "Agreed." Then she glared at Juliet. "We should be thankful Ophelia gives with so little regard for herself. We all benefit from compassion." Then she swept her around the table. "But as it stands, being kind to a duke could have great benefit to Ophelia. Even if he doesn't marry her himself, he could help her to make a strong match. Which is why…" Now she glared at Adrianna. "We're not going to tell Papa about the kiss."

"Thank you," Ophelia answered, reaching for Cordelia's hand.

But Bianca shook her head. "Wouldn't it be better to just tell Papa and have him force a match? Then you'd be married to a duke."

Ophelia shook her head. "I don't want a husband who has been forced." She thought of all her dreams.

How her match came to be was as important to her as the end result of marriage.

"Besides," Juliet shrugged. "Papa isn't even titled. He might fail to force a duke into anything and then Ophelia would be without a husband or a connection."

"So it's agreed," Cordelia said. "We don't tell Papa and we allow Ophelia to aid the duke."

Ophelia frowned. "If he even comes back. At this point, I'm not certain he will." And despite her determination in the wee hours of the night to help the man, she wasn't at all sure she wanted him to. Even wounded, or maybe because of the wounds he bore, he had great potential to hurt her. Her stomach flipped. Perhaps instead of planning how to help him, she should pray he never came back.

CHAPTER SIX

THE WIND WHIPPED at the carriage, rattling the wood. Though the rain had passed, heavy gusts had clearly blown away the storm and most everything else. Chase had passed two barns that had collapsed in the high wind, and unease set in his stomach like a stone.

First, he couldn't shake the feeling he wasn't where he belonged, and he'd debated turning back a dozen or so times. Second, he had some vague worry about Ophelia and the wind, though he knew she was tucked safely inside her house built of stone, he felt like he should be next to her even now, making sure she was safe.

One damned kiss and he was a mooning fool. But it was more than the kiss. He'd been mad for her after it, yes, but their conversation in the hall…it had shifted something inside him. He'd told her things he hadn't spoken of in years.

He scrubbed his face. He needed to go back. Whatever had happened between himself and Ophelia, he needed to explore it. Then he let out a grunt as he dropped his hands. He could add Ophelia to the list of growing problems for which he had no answers.

But one certainty had become clear. Whatever information he sought, it was not at the Baron Balstead's party. And just knowing that made him relax back in his seat.

"Yer Grace," his driver called. "I think ye should see this." The carriage squeaked to a halt.

Chase didn't bother to wait for the door to be opened. He clicked the latch himself and swung out of the vehicle. They were perched above a decent cliff that descended down into a river. A bridge connected the land to the other side but several travelers stood before the entrance, not crossing to the other side.

He started for the men collected at the opening. A farmer sat on top of his wagon, another traveler stood nearby on foot and three finely dressed men sat on horseback. He narrowed his gaze. Why did they look familiar? He grimaced, trying to place them, as the three men approached.

"What's happened?" He asked, still not sure where he knew them from.

The one closest to him swung down. "Bridge is out, damaged from the storm." His tone was flat and his words clipped as he looked at Chase with his brow set low over his eyes.

Chase assessed the bridge. From what he could see it looked intact.

The second man removed his hat and swept a hand through his golden hair. He couldn't have been more opposite from the other fellow. His blond hair glinted in the sun as his blue eyes flashed. "Looks all right from here but several of the boards washed out. Whole sections. It will take days to repair."

The third one grunted, "We're already late. At this rate, we'll miss all of Balstead's party."

Chase gave them a sharp glare, his memory clicking into place. These men had been at the club with Balstead the night the man had invited him. "You're heading to Balstead's too."

The last man swung down from his mount. "Viscount of Dashlane, at your service. Nice to see you again, Your Grace."

"The Indecent Duke?" the blond crowed. "Here in Seabridge Gate. What an odd place to meet again but a welcome surprise. I am the Earl of Crestwood and this is my perfectly awful friend, the Baron of Craven. It's a pleasure to finally meet you."

Chase jerked his chin. "What brings you along this road to reach Balstead's?"

"My country estate is just south of here. We made our way there to check on my holdings first and were delayed by a few issues." Crestwood gave a shrug. "Now it appears we'll be delayed again."

"Shame," Dashlane murmured. "There's nothing but milkmaids and fishermen's daughters in these parts. Nothing a man could sink his teeth into."

Chase shifted on his feet. The man's words rang vulgar to his ear and caused his stomach to sour. "How will you get to the party?"

Craven's brow furrowed. "It'll take days to find another river crossing. The only option is by boat but it will mean buying new horses on the other side."

Crestwood shrugged. "That's all right. It'll be an adventure and well worth the trouble. We'll head back down to Seabridge Gate and find someone to charter us north. Maybe."

Bloody hell and feck, Chase swore softly under his breath. These men were going to head straight to Ophelia. "Why don't I travel with you?" He had absolutely no intention of going to Balstead's and even less inclination to get on a boat, but he'd see these men safely off to their party—and away from Ophelia.

And if any of them attempted to touch Ophelia… well, they were going to answer to him.

Ophelia made her way down the rocky path, breathing in the fresh air. The wind whipped her bonnet but at least it had dried most of the water so the mud had dried. Juliet picked a path behind her. "Slow down. Why are you in such a hurry?"

Ophelia didn't quite know how to answer that. As the eldest woman in the family, she often performed the duties of mistress and one of them was going to the market to pick out their cuts of meat. "It's a beautiful day and I feel like a good walk."

Which was true. She enjoyed the exercise and fresh air as well as the relationships she had with many of the villagers. Seabridge Gate was located in an inlet, with lots of colorfully painted buildings dotting the shore. A main street led down to the docks where her father spent much of his time. The village itself was built around a square and it gave the town a lovely spot to congregate. At the very end, stood a large, steepled church. She stopped for a moment admiring her home. She loved it here. Always had.

Then why did she feel this driving urge to find… something else? Romance, love, marriage. Why couldn't Seabridge Gate be enough?

From across the square, four men caught her attention. Something in the way one of them stood, legs apart, reminded her of the duke. But that couldn't be. He'd gone, left for his house party, his return uncertain.

But thinking of him did remind her of the real reason she was in such a hurry to come down to the village. She'd wondered, would the village seem the same after her first brush with romance?

"Gads, Ophelia, you nearly sprinted here," Juliet puffed, tucking a stray lock of her blonde hair back into her bonnet. "I'll ask again. What is your hurry?"

But Ophelia was spared answering. Juliet caught sight of the four men and she straightened, staring across the square. "They're new."

"Indeed they are," Ophelia answered, reaching for her sister's hand. "Come. We'll miss the butcher if we don't hurry."

Juliet harrumphed. "That's hardly fair. You got to kiss a duke. Can't we at least accidentally on purpose bump into them? You're not the only Moorish who is getting on in years. At twenty, I need to find a husband soon."

"We'll accidentally on purpose bump into them after we go to the butcher. I can't go home without meat." But secretly she hoped they'd be gone by the time she finished shopping. It turned out the village felt even better for her brush with the duke. The interaction had left her vulnerable and the familiarity of this place was exactly the balm she needed, minus the strangers, of course.

Ophelia and Juliet started across the square, cutting an angle toward the butcher shop. Ophelia pulled her sister along, hoping to hurry before anyone saw them.

But just as they walked almost across, a voice rang out over the square. "Pardon me, ladies," a deep male voice called. "But I wonder if you might help us."

Drat. They'd been caught.

For a moment, she considered ignoring the caller. Could she pretend she hadn't heard?

But Juliet stopped, digging her heels into the soft dirt. "Of course," she called back. "How can we help?"

Ophelia shot her sister a glare but Juliet didn't pay her attention as she waved to the approaching men. Ophelia followed her sister's gaze and froze in place as Chase's green eyes connected with hers. One of the men was indeed her duke. A lump formed in her throat. What was Chase doing here? Should she run? Or was this her chance to help heal her wounded duke?

CHAPTER SEVEN

Even with the bonnet partially obscuring her face, Chase could see the surprise that widened her eyes. While he'd have preferred to reunite back at her home, he'd not leave her alone with these men for all his land in England.

He didn't trust Crestwood in particular. While Craven was quiet, which lent him an air of dangerous mystery, he'd not actually uttered much that was disrespectful either. And Dashlane was an exuberant fellow who liked fun. But Crestwood? His rakish streak ran deep. The man talked of little else besides chasing skirts—all skirts, older women to young, rich to poor. He seemed to have a taste for truly beautiful ladies, which meant his interest would likely be in Ophelia.

He supposed he was making a rather uneducated

judgment. He'd only known the men a few hours, other than their one other meeting, but they'd ridden in his carriage on the way back to Seabridge Gate and the filth that had dribbled from Crestwood's mouth had made Chase's teeth clench. Dashlane and Craven had only been a little better. He wasn't sure when he'd become this man, disgusted with their loose morals.

Crestwood faltered in his step. "Christ," he muttered. "That one on the left is stunning. I wonder what color her hair is under that bonnet."

Chase clenched his hand, fisting his fingers into his palm. Crestwood referred to Ophelia. If the man said anything crass, Chase would punch him before the earl even knew it was coming.

"Their clothes are fine, they're not milkmaids or fishermen's daughters," Dashlane grinned. "And they might be amenable to spending time with titled lords. They'll be looking for husbands, but what they don't know…"

Chase's nostrils flared. Never mind that he'd done the exact same thing last night. No other man was touching Ophelia, that he was certain of. Remorse over his own behavior the night before weighed down his chest.

Crestwood stopped two feet in front of the ladies

and gave a bow. "Pleasure to make your acquaintance, ladies. I'm the Earl of Crestwood."

Chase clenched his teeth as Ophelia's sister giggled. He couldn't remember her bloody name. He had to learn them.

Crestwood made the last of the introductions, even announcing Chase. Both Ophelia and the other one dropped into dutiful curtseys. "Your Grace," Ophelia murmured, her voice dropping low on the last note which added a definite chill to the courtesy. Then she rose. "I am Miss Moorish, as is my sister. Apologies, gentlemen but we have an urgent errand to run. What might you need help with?"

Chase relaxed a bit as Ophelia's cool tone extended to the other men. She might sound cold because she was angry with him, but she was sending a clear message to these other men to keep away and he was grateful.

"There's no need to rush, Ophelia." The other one giggled, stepping forward. "Pleased to make your acquaintance," she said as she held out her hand.

"Juliet." Ophelia also moved ahead placing a restrictive hand on her sister's arm. "We don't have time to dally."

"We'll be quick then." Crestwood took Juliet's hand, then placed a light kiss on her glove. The

WHEN ONLY AN INDECENT DUKE WILL DO

gesture was long and drawn out and not at all fast. "We're in need of a boat to carry us north."

"Why?" Ophelia asked, giving Juliet a long stare.

"The bridge is washed out," Chase answered, cutting in front of the other men to stand next to her. He intended to send a clear message as well.

She looked up at him. "Is that why you've returned?"

"Returned?" Dashlane asked. "You didn't mention you knew such lovely ladies here in Seabridge Gate during our carriage ride."

Chase straightened. "I didn't." Then he placed a hand under Ophelia's elbow. "I'll escort you ladies on your errand and then perhaps your father can help these gentlemen charter a ship out of Seabridge Gate."

"Excellent," Crestwood answered. "We can all go on your errand."

Chase stopped, drawing in a deep breath, trying to control his intense dislike for this man. Crestwood needed to leave. Immediately. "Perhaps you should secure potential lodging? In case you can't leave town tonight."

Ophelia gave a quick nod. "That's a good idea. It's a difficult time of day to reach my father."

Chase turned, taking Ophelia with him. "We should go before it's too late."

She nibbled her lip, looking up at him. "Will you be going with them? On the boat?"

He lightly squeezed her elbow. Now was not the time to share that his parents had died in these very waters and he'd never set foot in a boat as long as he lived. "No. I'll stay here until I return home."

Her head cocked to the side. "Then I'd appreciate your escort to the butcher, Your Grace."

He gave a quick nod. "I'd be happy to." Then he turned to her sister, "Come along, Juliet. We'll see our new friends in just a bit."

Juliet gave an audible sigh but did as he commanded. A quick glance back confirmed the three men glared at him. He didn't care. Let them glare. Just as long as they weren't anywhere near the Moorish sisters, Ophelia in particular, they could hate his guts.

OPHELIA GLANCED OVER AT CHASE, his fingers sure and strong on her elbow as she continued to bite her lip. Why was he escorting her to the butcher? Why wasn't he going to his party? Why— She stopped. There was little point in letting all these questions swirl about now, they weren't likely to be answered.

"Do you think your father would permit me to

stay again?" Chase asked, his chin dropping close to her ear.

She turned to look at him, aware of how close their faces were. "I'm sure he would." She drew in a steadying breath and inadvertently inhaled his fresh sandalwood scent. "For how long?"

He turned down the side street where the butcher was located. "I'm not certain. But I didn't know if I'd be welcomed back after last night."

She stopped then, Juliet nearly running into her back. "I didn't tell him, if that's what you're asking."

Juliet tapped both their shoulders. "We know, though. Adrianna caught you."

Chase muttered something under his breath that she was fairly certain was a curse word.

"Perhaps." She looked back at her sister, giving her a glare. "It would be best if you didn't stay after all."

"Why not?" He scrunched his brow, staring down at her.

She shook her head, wondering if the man was daft. She hadn't thought so up to this point but the answer seemed obvious to her. "My sisters are not the best secret keepers. If my father finds out…"

He shrugged. "We'll deal with that when it comes."

Well that wasn't helpful and only added to the

questions she was trying to quiet in her thoughts. She let out a small noise of dissent. "How lovely."

He raised a brow as they entered the shop. "Most women would be thrilled to catch a duke."

"I'm not most women," she answered, moving ahead of him toward the counter. The truth was, the entire conversation had her at her wit's end. Had she wanted to help this man? She'd suspected that was a silly notion, he scrambled all her plans whenever he was near.

He chuckled as she left his side and approached the butcher.

She ordered the meat, though Ophelia had little memory of what or why when their small party exited the shop, Chase once again stationed at her elbow. Though they didn't make it far.

Outside the shop stood the three lords that Chase had been with in the square. Chase stopped short, Ophelia stopping too and Juliet, once again, bumping into their backs.

"We've got a bit of a problem," Crestwood said, frowning at the possessive hand Chase had on her elbow. "The inn is full."

Chase paused and she wondered if he were going to answer. Was it her place to? But then he cleared his throat. "Where are your holdings that you came to check on?"

Crestwood narrowed his gaze. "More than a day's ride south of here. And then we'll have that much more to sail in order to reach Dover."

"Perhaps," Chase pulled her a touch closer, "the house party just isn't in your future."

"Is it in yours?" Crestwood stepped a bit closer.

"No," Chase bit back, hostility that Ophelia didn't quite understand crackling in the air.

But Juliet gave the tiniest giggle behind her. "Oh. This is delicious. You lucky thing, you."

What did that mean? She glanced over her shoulder at her sister. Then back at the three men before them. All three were assessing her with various degrees of interest. Their eyes roved her body, her face, her basket.

"If not the party then where will you go?" Crestwood asked, running a hand through his wavy blond hair and flashing her a bright smile.

"Back to London," Chase grit out.

"Really," Crestwood shifted. "You won't stay here?"

Chase's fingers tightened on her elbow. "That's none of your business."

"I disagree." Crestwood said before his gaze flipped to her again. "Miss Moorish. You mentioned that you could introduce us to your father. Could we trouble you to do so now?"

Chase gave a rumble in his chest that sounded near like a growl. The sound, rather than frightening, however, seemed to settle deep in her belly and cause little tendrils of pleasure to go dancing in her most private of areas. Oh dear. What was she going to do now?

CHAPTER EIGHT

Chase wanted to bash Crestwood's head with his fist. If he were lucky, blood would squirt from the man's perfectly straight nose. He gave a mean grin at the thought. He could see Crestwood sizing up Ophelia. He'd be interested in her anyhow. She was stunning and her body... He clenched his teeth together. But with Chase having laid claim, well, he'd piqued the man's interest further. Chase was sure of it.

Drawing in a deep breath, Chase attempted to calm the surge of jealous rage that had risen up, making it difficult to even think. He'd never responded like this before, the feeling was almost primal.

Ophelia gave a delicate cough. "I can try, my lord.

It's half tide, which means he's likely doing rounds on all the ships getting ready to leave the harbor."

Craven gave a grumble. "If we don't find him that means we can't board a boat until at least tomorrow."

Crestwood wiggled his brows. "We'll have to find somewhere to stay then, besides the inn. Does anyone have any ideas?"

"Oh," Juliet called from the back. "I'm sure we can help you."

Chase looked back at Juliet, he hoped his face properly portrayed how much he wanted her to cease talking. She caught his glare and took a half step back, her lips pressing together as her eyes widened.

"We'll see if there is a house in the village where you can stay," Chase pushed out between gritted teeth. "In fact, since we're unlikely to find Mr. Moorish, perhaps we should secure lodging for our fine friends first."

"Fine friends?" Crestwood repeated. "I thought so in the carriage, but now I'm beginning to wonder."

That was fair, Chase supposed. In his defense, he'd actually said little. "Miss Moorish," he looked down into Ophelia's kind, chocolate-brown stare. Everything about her eyes warmed him on the inside. "Do we know where these men might be able to stay?"

Ophelia's nose twitched, just a bit, as she considered his question. "There is an empty cottage at the back of the square that my father owns. I'm sure he'd allow them to stay there."

Chase gave a tight nod. He'd prefer to get these men on a boat and out of Seabridge Gate as quickly as he could but at least they weren't staying at the manor with the family.

"And you must come for dinner," Juliet called again.

"Excellent idea," Crestwood answered. "Tonight?"

Ophelia shook her head. "I'm sorry, my lord, but I doubt it. With high tide so late, my father isn't likely to be home this evening until very late."

"Tomorrow then." Juliet actually put her hand on his shoulder to lift up and see the other men better. He didn't have any strong feelings about any of Ophelia's sisters but if she spoke one more word, he might have to stuff his cravat in her mouth.

"They are trying to get to Ipswich, Miss Moorish," Chase said, giving her the eye again. Why wasn't she getting the hint to stop? These men were the worst sort of rakes and they needed to leave this sleepy village at once.

"We can delay one more day for such an invitation," Crestwood volunteered.

"Now see here," Dashlane interrupted.

"What?" Craven asked, his voice dropping dangerously low.

Chase looked back at Juliet. The woman was mad and he'd like to throttle her, but instead he'd have to protect her from these men. Because somewhere between that broken bridge and right now, he'd made a decision. He'd marry Ophelia. He couldn't stand the thought of another man touching her. Later he'd worry about what a disappointment he was likely to be as a husband.

"We'll make it for the second half of the debauchery," Crestwood said to his companions.

Ophelia sucked in a sharp breath. Debauchery? What did that mean? She looked at Chase whose jaw had tightened to the point of appearing as though it might shatter. But a whole new series of questions had started thrumming through her thoughts. Was he also planning debauchery at this party? Was that his intent with her as well?

She took a half step away from him but he pulled his arm tighter to his body.

"That's enough, Crestwood." But it wasn't Chase who spoke but Craven. "There are ladies present." Craven's gaze settled on Juliet, who blushed furiously.

Crestwood looked back at them, his mouth tightening as he gave a quick bow. "Apologies, ladies."

"Let's find your father," Chase said as he started leading her down the street. "Juliet, if you'd kindly take my other arm."

Her sister dutifully stepped up next to Chase, though she gave a long look back at Craven. Ophelia understood that Chase didn't want Juliet being escorted by one of those other men but she was beginning to wonder if he was any better.

She wasn't saving this man from anything. Her instinct to run had been much more apt. They walked down toward the docks, and she turned to the left. Her father had a small office in one of the buildings located on the shore. He could watch all the ships coming in and out and captains could easily report to him.

The building was painted a fun shade of dark red with large black-trimmed, multi-paned windows. A bell hung above the door and its cheerful call had given her and her sisters hours of entertainment as children.

Seabridge Gate was technically a peninsula

between two rivers. But the mainland of England jutted out just beyond Seabridge Gate's shore on both sides, providing a uniquely protected harbor and her father a booming business providing them all with a wonderful life. She entered the shop to find her father's clerk behind his desk. "Hello, Mr. Burton," she said as the entire group filed into the office.

Mr. Burton looked up, surprise lighting his gaze. "Ophelia, Juliet. Good to see you. To what do I owe this…" He glanced at the four men. "Surprise?"

Ophelia gave Chase a hesitant glance before she looked back to her father's old clerk. "His Grace was a guest of ours last evening."

"Interesting," Crestwood muttered behind her.

Ophelia continued as though he hadn't spoken. Weary as she was of Chase, she knew she was relatively safe in his company and she'd stay close to him while with Crestwood. "These other lords are trapped in town because the bridge to the north was damaged in the storm. They were hoping to speak with Papa about passage and the use of the cottage on Mayfair Street."

Mr. Burton nodded. "I'm sure you know your father is currently making the rounds. But I can give you the key to the cottage and Mr. Moorish will most certainly visit the gentlemen there on his way home."

"Thank you, Mr. Burton," Ophelia answered. "That is an excellent plan."

Chase leaned down close to her ear. "I'll see both you and Juliet home."

It was on the tip of her tongue to say that wasn't necessary but a quick glance back over her shoulder, and she swallowed the words, giving a terse nod instead. With the wolf Crestwood just behind her, it seemed prudent to accept his offer.

They made their way back out of the shop and down the coastal street and then took a right onto Mayfair. Though the cottage was empty currently, it was used by captains who were in Seabridge Gate on longer stopovers and so it was kept clean and well-stocked. "You'll find everything you need in the cottage," she said to the men. "There is food as well but you'll likely enjoy dinner out at the tavern."

The three men said little as she stopped in front of the house and unlocked the door. Stepping inside, she motioned for the other members of the party to follow. The cottage was cheerfully decorated in a nautical theme. Ophelia had done a great deal of the work herself.

"When you said unoccupied cottage…" Dashlane

started. "I thought you meant unused and untouched. This is…"

"Far better than the last four inns we stayed in," Craven finished. "By a magnitude of ten."

"Thank you," she answered. "I think." She tapped her chin. "I've never actually stayed in an inn so I don't know how good or bad they actually are. But we use this cottage regularly to give our captains a homier place to stay if they are in port for more than a night or two."

Chase looked at her then. "You've never stayed in an inn?"

She shook her head. "My father's work demands his constant attention and with my mother gone…"

"Aunts?" he asked.

She shrugged, looking at a painting of the very harbor they'd just left. Her father's relationship with his brother was fair but he didn't approve of his sister-in-law's parenting practices. He'd never wanted to leave his daughters in her care. "My father hasn't sent me to the countess yet."

Crestwood cleared his throat. "It's very nice what you've done for us, both of you."

Ophelia nodded but she noted Juliet's blush. She'd been irritated with her sister when she'd invited these men for dinner, but she understood why Juliet had. Apparently, she wasn't the only

Moorish sister starving for a bit of fun and romance. "We're always happy to help guests of Seabridge Gate," she answered. "If for some reason my father does not stop by on his way home, I'll see that he does first thing in the morning. In the meantime, there are two bedrooms upstairs and a third in the back, just down the hall. To reach the town square again, you only need continue up Mayfair Street."

Juliet gave a small curtsy. "We'll send a maid over as well to make sure you are comfortable." She looked up at the ceiling, tapping her chin. "Miss Kitteridge lives in the village so it would be an easy assignment for her. Is that all right, Ophelia?"

"Of course," she answered.

"Thank you," Craven replied, giving her sister a long look.

It was innocent enough but Ophelia straightened, ready to defend her sister. She faced the lords who became their unexpected guests. "But let's be clear that Miss Kitteridge is here for cleaning and shopping only." She pressed her lips together as her face tightened. "And dinner tomorrow night will be a friendly event meant for introductions and polite conversation." She turned to her sister. "Please step outside for just a moment."

Juliet frowned but did as her sister commanded. Then she turned to face the four lords who had landed in Seabridge Gate. She met each of their gazes, including Chase. "None of you are to do anything untoward involving my staff or my family. Just so that you're aware, the benefit of growing up in the country is that I'm adept at firing a pistol or a rifle. I'll shoot you out of this town if I have to. There will be no debauchery in my village."

Not one of them said a word. While Crestwood wore a look of surprise, his eyes widening, Craven's face remained unchanged. She didn't bother to look at Dashlane, instead focusing on Chase. He had the decency to look at the floor, his features tight with what she assumed was regret. She didn't say another word as she turned and left.

CHAPTER NINE

CHASE WATCHED her walk down the steps and he started to follow but Crestwood grabbed his arm. "You wanted to protect them," Crestwood said as Chase turned back to look at the man.

"Yes," he said, his chest tightening. "I've grown weary of the so-called delights in this world and those women are..." He paused, picturing Ophelia. "More wholesome than any I've met in a long time." Then he straightened to his full height. "I think it best that you gentlemen continue your journey north without delay. I also am quite good with a pistol and I've no intention of allowing the debauchery to spread to Seabridge Gate."

Crestwood gave a jerky nod. "I understand, but I must tell you, her delivery was much better."

Craven stared at him for a moment before he cleared his throat. "Will you marry Ophelia?"

"Yes," he answered, surprising even himself with how little hesitation he felt. In fact, it was the first right thing he'd said in ages. "If she'll have me. After today, I'm not so certain." But he was going to try. For the first time in what felt like years, the fog surrounding his path had cleared. He knew exactly who he wanted to be, where he wanted to be, and what he desired for his future.

And that was next to Miss Ophelia Moorish.

He rubbed his hand through his hair. If only he'd come to that conclusion last night. This entire thing might have been easier. In fact, he'd likely already be engaged. Bloody idiot, that's what he was.

Dashlane grimaced. "Sorry about that." Then he cleared his throat. "But we might attend that dinner if for no other reason than to thank our hosts. This little house is so cheerful that I almost feel a deep regret—" He stopped. "But I can assure you that I will be on my best behavior."

Craven nodded. "As will I."

Crestwood grimaced but said nothing and Chase decided he didn't care. One man he could handle. If Crestwood tried to misbehave with any of the Moorish sisters, he could take the man. With that in mind, he turned on his heel and started after Ophelia.

Reaching the square, he saw them start down a path that was dappled with trees and rocks. Surely it was a shortcut to the house so that they didn't need to take the road. He picked up speed and caught up to them as they crested the first hill.

Juliet was talking nonstop. "Did you see them? They were so handsome. Crestwood is the leader, don't you think? And Dashlane…what a dashing name."

Ophelia lifted her skirts as they continued to climb up the hill. "No one likes a romantic story better than me but those men…" She paused, her feet slowing. "They are not the stuff of romantic fantasy, Juliet. They are nightmares."

Juliet sniffed. "That's easy for you to say. The duke's interest in you is—"

Ophelia raised her hand. "Irrelevant."

"I beg to differ," he said, announcing his presence behind them. Both women jumped.

"What are you doing?" Ophelia huffed and then started moving again, pulling her sister along.

"I told you that I would escort you home." He had every intention of keeping Ophelia in his sights now.

Ophelia didn't stop. "That is entirely unnecessary."

"It isn't," he said, easily matching their pace despite Ophelia's attempts to speed up.

"It is," she answered, stopping on the trail and spinning back around to him. "When you consider that you and your friends are the most dangerous things in Seabridge Gate."

He winced. Her point was sound. "They are not my friends."

Her hands came to her hips. "Will you deny then that you are dangerous?"

He shifted his weight, looking to the ground. "I owe you an explanation."

"You don't." She shook her head. "I've pieced it all together myself. But I would appreciate it if you'd return to the cottage and stay with the other men. I won't tell my father but I'd rather you not stay in our home."

Juliet gasped and his teeth snapped together. He drew in a long breath, choosing his next words very carefully. "Juliet. Would you be so kind as to walk far enough ahead of us that you can still see us but that we have a chance to talk?"

Juliet looked at her sister and Ophelia shifted again, her fists clenching in her skirts. "Fine," she answered for her sister. "Go ahead, Juliet."

He sighed a small bit of relief. At least he could

plead his case. What her answer would be, he still couldn't say.

OPHELIA WAITED, her toe tapping as Juliet strolled ahead. Nothing but the sound of the ocean and the chirping of birds filled the silence that hung between them.

"Well," she asked, clasping her hands together. The single word had come out harshly but her feelings of hurt and betrayal added an edge to her voice. He'd known she was smitten and he'd kissed her just for fun, not returning her romantic interest.

"I already told you that I lost my parents."

He reached for her hand but she didn't take it. "You did," she said, facing the ocean to stare at the wave. She could see the cool blue off in the distance, from this spot on the hill path. "And I felt sorry for you. Thought maybe I could help—" She stopped, clamping her lips shut.

"Ophelia, you are so kind." He stepped closer, touching her arm. "Thank you."

"I was wrong," She looked at him, her face taut with the tension that thrummed through her entire body. "You only wanted my kisses. Maybe you wanted more, I don't know."

"Why do you think that?" He lightly brushed his fingers back and forth along her sleeve.

It was a light touch meant to soothe and she tried to ignore the warmth that spread from that touch. "You left." She took another step back. "To attend a party where you hoped to engage in—" Heat filled her cheeks as she took another step in retreat. Unfortunately her heel hit a rock and she started to fall backward.

She flailed her hands, but Chase was quick and lunged forward, catching her and dragging her against his chest.

The moment she came into contact with the hard muscles of his body her own shivered in response. She spread her hands over his chest, heat rising in her cheeks.

"I've been searching for what thing would fill my life," he whispered close to her ear. "My parents died in a boat wreck and the truth was, I should have gone with them. I told them I was staying home because I needed to return to Oxford, but the truth was I wanted to tup one of the maids." He shuddered against her, the memory clearly causing him pain. She found her arms sliding up about his neck. "I should have been with them instead of fooling around with some girl who meant nothing. That seems to be all I am good at. Meaningless dalliances."

Her heart ached for him and she began to understand his penchant for debauchery…or she thought she might. Meeting his eyes, she pressed her lips together. "You're wrong. I don't blame you for being wrong; I don't know how I might have survived a loss like yours. I had my sisters and my father when my mother passed. But you shouldn't have been on that boat and if your parents could talk, they'd thank their lucky stars that you wished to tup a maid."

He gave a short barking laugh as he slowly righted them, but kept her in his arms. "I'd never thought about it that way."

"They'd want you to live, to be a duke, to…" She hesitated.

He bent his head down, touching his forehead to hers. "To marry a nice girl who would keep me from debauchery and have my babies and help carry on the family name."

She couldn't help it. That part of her that had been wishing to hear those words jolted inside her, sending a shower of excitement all through her body. "I suppose they would."

His fingers spread on her back. "I want you to be that woman, Ophelia."

Clutching about his neck, she hung on as she fought the wave of longing that rose inside her. It was a nice proposal as far as those sorts of things went. He'd bared his hurt, he'd asked for her help. Two things that made her most happy. But it lacked one crucial ingredient. This was her one opportunity to have a grand adventure...falling in love. He'd talked of her suitability, what a nice girl she was. But there had not been a hint of affection that had tinted his words. "It's a lovely offer," she whispered as she tried to loosen her grip and back out of his arms, but he held firm.

"I'm not sure that means yes." He frowned, his brows drawing together.

She shook her head. "It doesn't."

The frown deepened. "Are you angry that I kissed you?"

"No." She stopped trying to pull away. "The kiss was wonderful. The single best moment of my life." How did she explain that the kiss they'd shared held all the romance and passion she'd dreamed of, read about, wished for all her life? And his proposal was decidedly lacking in that same emotion.

"I don't think I understand." Then his brows lifted. "You're upset about the party. Or about my past being so...colorful."

She cocked her head considering his words. "Maybe. In fairness, I tend to paint my life with a romantic brush and when you left this morning...I realized this wasn't a grand gesture on your part. But

I still thought to help you with your grief. You haven't had anyone for that." She drew in a deep breath. "But when I learned you left me to go tup whomever you planned to tup, well...I've come to the conclusion that I'm not the woman for the job. I'm no match for such an experienced lord."

He squeezed his eyes shut. "You are better for the job than any woman I've ever met."

That surprised her and she had to confess the tiniest seed of hope bloomed in her chest. It might be foolish on her part, likely was, but she wondered if she could help him still. And by some miracle, perhaps, in helping him, real love could develop between them. She sucked in her breath. That was an adventure of a different kind but an adventure still.

CHAPTER TEN

CHASE SAT in a dark corner of the library watching the door. Mr. Moorish hadn't arrived home until after eleven and then he'd begged forgiveness from Chase but he was dead tired and requested they speak in the morning.

Chase had agreed.

Mr. Moorish had rubbed his eyes and muttered something about an unusual proliferation of lords.

Chase had winced and choked back a laugh in the same moment. Mr. Moorish was absolutely correct and even worse, they were lords of the worst ilk. Though, he might count himself as a recently reformed rake. He had no desire to touch anyone other than Ophelia. And he wanted to touch her often and everywhere.

Which was why he now sat in the library. He happened to know this was her favorite room and eventually she'd come in search of a book. Perhaps not tonight but as he wasn't likely to sleep anyhow, he might as well wait on the off chance she arrived.

He should be exhausted. He'd been up most of the night last night and had travelled all day. But he'd never been less inclined to sleep in his life. Every nerve ending was ablaze as he remembered the feel of Ophelia pressed against him when she'd tripped that afternoon.

He pictured her lush lips, her sparkling eyes, the feel of her curves. While she hadn't said yes to his proposal, she hadn't said no either. And, former rake that he was, he had decided to use her attraction to him against her. He knew when a woman wanted him…she did…and how to touch her in all the ways that would override her better judgment.

His morals pricked at the thought. This sinful behavior was what he'd been running from most of his life. He seduced first and considered the consequences later, but in this case, he didn't think he was being rash. The consequence was marriage to one of the most wholesome of people. Something that was sure to be good for him.

A rustling by the door pulled him from his

thoughts and he sat straighter in his chair, squinting his eyes toward the entrance.

Ophelia appeared to float into the room, a gauzy night rail skimming down her body as she held a single candle aloft.

He caught his breath as he noted her loosely braided hair that cascaded over one creamy shoulder. She appeared almost magical, as though she'd risen from one of the fairy tales she loved so much and he stared in wonder as her fingertips skimmed along the spines of several books. It must be a habit of hers for he'd witnessed her do the same thing the previous night, but it was no less entrancing.

Her fingers were long and tapered, her touch exceedingly gentle, her gaze dreamy... Or was he imagining that?

He nearly laughed to himself, thinking that Ophelia was rewriting his own preferences because the library was fast becoming the most erotic place in the world.

Slowly, he pushed up from the chair. She stopped, setting down her candle and then pulling a book from the shelf. Ophelia cracked open the binding and skimmed a few pages before she put the title away again. "Which of you will help me sleep?" she asked, tilting her head up to scan the shelves.

"I will," he answered, moving into the circle of her light the candle shown.

She gave a yelp and spun about to face him but he was quick and circled her waist with his hands to steady her.

She frowned. "You frightened me."

"Apologies, my sweet. You told me last night to do my pacing in the library since I couldn't sleep." He flashed her his best smile. "I was attempting to guard your sleep."

First surprise flitted across her features, widening her eyes, and then understanding softened them, her lips curving up into a smile. "I did say that, didn't I?" She shook her head. "I couldn't sleep either."

"Why not?" He fitted her against his frame as she looked away at the shelves of books.

"It was an interesting day."

His eyebrows rose as he bent his head closer to hers. "Why is that?"

One of her brows quirked up in response. "Let's see. A duke asked me to marry him, several more lords arrived in town, my sisters are absolutely atwitter and…" She held up a single finger, "My father seems oblivious to it all."

"Does he?" he asked, sliding the tips of his fingers up her back, the curve of it causing his body to tighten. "He knows the other men are here. He mentioned it."

She shook her head. "He's always had his head in the clouds…or more accurately, in books. I know the feeling but I'd like to think that I quickly come back to reality. And the reality is my sisters and I are in danger."

"No, that isn't true," he whispered, letting his breath tickle the skin of her neck. "I would never let anything happen to you and, as your husband and a duke, I would make sure those men behaved."

She shivered and he knew his touch was working. "But who will protect me from you?"

CHASE CLENCHED his teeth as her words settled over him. It was an excellent question. He used his middle finger to trace the curve of her delicate shoulder. "You don't need protecting from me, love. I want to tuck you by my side and keep you safe always."

"Very pretty words," she murmured, her breath catching as his finger traced the inside of her arm, just grazing the flesh of her breast. "But even in this moment you are compromising my—" She stopped as he reached her bare wrist and then ran his fingers across her open palm. Her breathing was shallow as she looked down at their hands.

"I'm not compromising. I am convincing."

Her lashes fluttered closed. "Convincing me of what…exactly?"

Leaning down, he placed a light kiss just behind her ear. The candlelight flickered off her skin as his lips caressed her silky flesh. "That I can make you happy as a husband. Keep you content." Then he kissed a trail down her neck and across her collarbone.

"I've no doubt that you can teach me all sorts of delicious things." She brought her hands up to grasp his biceps, her head tilting back as victory sang in his veins. "My concerns involve our emotional bond and possibly your fidelity."

He loosened the string of the night rail about her neck. "My fidelity is not a concern, Ophelia. I swear to you, you will find me in your bed every night. I wish to leave my past self behind and start a much brighter future with you." And then he kissed the skin of her chest, now exposed.

She dug her fingers into his arms. "That is comforting."

"Let me show you how good it could be." He continued to kiss over the cloth, blazing a trail to the peak of her breast. They were as full as he'd imagined them to be and cupping one, he kissed her nipple then sucked it into his mouth.

Her gasp and then moan said all he needed to know. But then her fingers, which had been gripping him tightly, started to push him away. "I shouldn't. We're not married or promised…what if—"

"Ophelia." He moved to the other nipple, bringing it into his mouth as she arched her back to meet his touch. He growled out his satisfaction as he showered attention on her other breast. "I'll not take your maidenhead, but I can show you how good it can be. Will you let me?"

She shook her head, starting to back up again. "Chase. I'm trying to decide the right path. I shouldn't allow what you're doing to color my thinking."

In answer, he ran his hand down her flat abdomen, the silky cotton of her night rail having warmed from their body heat. He slid his fingers between her legs, pressing lightly against her womanly flesh. Her sharp gasp let him know just how much she liked the touch as her knees buckled.

Wrapping his other hand below her behind, he held her up as he started sliding back and forth along her seam. She whimpered, her fingers digging into his neck. He increased the pressure as he lifted his head to take her lips in his own. She was careening toward her finish, her legs trembling against his. Much as he wanted to feel her break apart in his arms, this was a lesson on the benefits of making a rogue your own and he'd only just begun the lesson.

CHAPTER ELEVEN

A HOT, beautiful, agonizing passion curled from Ophelia's apex and spread through her body like fire. This was not a beautiful fairy tale, this was real and hot and so delicious that she could barely stand it.

"Would you like to know what else we could do?" Chase whispered in her ear, slowing his intimate caress.

"Don't stop," she managed to push out between breaths, digging her nails into the flesh of his neck. If she weren't careful, she'd leave marks.

He chuckled, the sound rumbling through her neck down her spine only adding to the pleasure. "Don't worry, love. What I do next will be so much better."

"Better?" When had her voice gotten so…needy?

It rasped with a high-pitch tone that practically begged for more.

"Better," he answered, suddenly lifting her off her feet and carrying her across the room to the settee. It was darker here away from the candle and she could only see his outline as he laid her down on the piece of furniture, his knees between hers, her legs falling as open as her night rail would allow.

Chase shrugged off his shirt, tossing the garment to the floor. "What are you doing?" she asked, her voice catching.

He gave a soft laugh, sounding both amused and just a touch deviant. "I am giving your nails more flesh to scratch."

She gasped then, starting to sit up. "Did I hurt you?"

Slowly, he began skimming the hem of her night clothes up her thighs. "Not to worry. I liked it. Very much." And then he pushed the fabric higher, exposing her naked lower half to his gaze. Heat filled her cheeks, but she consoled herself that he could neither see her blush or her womanly parts in the dark.

But he found her now-bare seam and ran the tip of his middle finger through her flesh as pleasure rioted through her. "Later. When you're more accustomed to lovemaking, we'll do this with a hundred candles lit all about. You look so beautiful in candlelight."

Her breath caught. How…romantic. "Really? You'd want to see me like this?"

"Ophelia," he groaned. "You have no idea how much I want to see, touch, taste every inch of you. I'm burning for you."

Her insides throbbed with pleasure. "When we light our hundred candles," she said, momentarily forgetting she hadn't agreed to marry him. "Can we cover the bed or couch or whatever it is in rose petals?"

He groaned. "Damn right we can."

She licked her lips as he pushed her night rail higher still, until the fabric gathered under her arms, exposing her abdomen and breasts. "It could be in the summer, with the doors open and a soft breeze coming in the room."

He didn't answer as he bent over her and took one of her now-bare nipples into his mouth. She gasped, digging her fingers into his scalp. "Oh," she breathed as his other hand lightly parted her female flesh. "Chase."

He started to kiss a trail down her stomach. "I love the sound of my name on your lips. Now tell me more of your fantasy. One hundred candles, rose petals, open doors and soft breeze. Will we be near the ocean?"

"Oh yes," she replied, his mouth tickling her lower stomach. "The sound of the waves will create a rhythm exactly like your hand and…" Was she saying too much?"

"I like the sound of that," he answered. "Very much. And I hate the open water."

She blinked, momentarily forgetting her pleasure or the fantasy. He'd taken the long route to Ipswich by the water, he'd mentioned he was searching for answers. He was still mourning his parents.

And then he moved lower, his tongue flicking against her tiny nub. Pleasure rocked through her. She'd been right, of course. He was too much rogue for her to handle. But she also realized she might be able to help him after all.

"Could we set up our candles, our bed, and our rose petals outside under the stars?" The words took forever to push out of her lips, her body twisting and turning inside from his touch.

"Yes," he said, lifting his head for just a moment. "That is a fabulous idea." Then he started again, increasing the pressure.

She dug her fingers into his shoulders, crying out as he slid a finger inside her body. He felt so good, she wondered if she'd die from the pleasure. If she did, it was a wonderful way to go.

CHASE SQUEEZED HIS EYES SHUT, trying to regain his sense of control. He'd started this seduction with a clear purpose but the longer he inhaled her, tasted her sweet strawberry nectar, touched the silky skin of her body, the less rational his thoughts became. First, she'd wrapped him in a delicious fantasy of making love under the open sky. Christ, the woman was a natural-born storyteller.

And then there was the actual passion she was capable of. Even now, her fingers left delightful little marks on his shoulders. He couldn't wait to see what sort of seductress she grew to be. Yesterday, she'd never even been kissed. Today, she was raking her nails along his skin and concocting elaborate seduction scenarios. But still, she needn't ever worry about his fidelity. This woman was everything he'd ever wanted all wrapped in one buxom little package.

His cock was near bursting as he slid his finger into her channel, the tight wet flesh making his vision blur. He shoved a hand into his breeches, needing almost no actual stimulation. She was enough. Her thighs quivered about his ears and the little mewling noises she made nearly tore him apart in pleasure. She sunk her fingernails even deeper into the skin of his shoulders as she panted, moaning out his name.

He didn't want to think of the scenes of carnality that he'd participated in or watched that had left him almost bored. But not this. He was going to soil his own damn pants at this rate.

And then she came apart, shuddering and shaking against his mouth. Christ. The indecent duke playing with himself as this woman turned him into a panting schoolboy barely even able to contain himself. As she bucked against him, he completely lost control, his own orgasm rocking through him. He groaned, her heady scent overwhelming his senses. If he'd been uncertain before, he knew it now. He was desperately in love with this woman. Crawling a few inches forward, he lay his head on her bare stomach.

Her fingers slid from his shoulders and into his hair, massaging his scalp in a slightly rough but very satisfying rhythm. "And when we're done, we'll fall asleep under the stars as the candles burn themselves out one by one."

He smiled. His legs were mostly hanging off the end of the settee, his shoulders crammed between her thighs, but he'd never been more comfortable in his life. "Can I stay up and watch them burn out?"

He felt the muscles of her stomach flex as she smiled. He'd never realized that before, that a smile could be felt so far down the body. He reached up and grasped her waist wanting to feel more of her as though he were learning the mysteries of life. "That's a delightful idea."

He skimmed his hand over her stomach. "Maybe that will be the time that I fill your belly with my baby. We'll start a family under the stars."

Her fingers stilled for a moment before they started again, her touch lighter. "Family?"

Was it him or did her voice sound more distant? Her fingers were still working through his hair and he closed his eyes, pushing away his worry. "We're going to have to buy a new home. I sold the property located on the ocean. It was one of the few that wasn't entailed."

She reached for his face then, cupping his cheeks in her hands and lifting his head so that their eyes met. He wondered when he might see her at her most lovely. Candlelight, daylight, threatening grown men with pistols. But right now, he was certain, this was the most enchanting she'd ever been. "We don't have to live near the ocean. Not if you don't like it."

She'd figured that out, had she? "I love your entire fantasy, so we'll see it come to life." He gave her a small grin. "Besides, it's time I got over my fear."

Her thumb grazed the corner of his lips. "If you truly want to, I'll help you."

"I do," he said as he started to climb higher up her body. Kissing her mouth, he lifted again, looking deep into her eyes. "With you there, maybe I can overcome the haunted feeling I get every time I look at the water."

"We'll go then." Placing her arms about his neck, she pulled him back down for another kiss. "If I can do one thing for you it's this."

One thing? She'd do far more than one, and he'd spend a lifetime giving everything he had to her. Didn't she understand that yet?

CHAPTER TWELVE

Ophelia frowned as he lay his head back down on her stomach. In a moment like this, she could almost believe that she didn't need Chase's love, just his touch. Surely her love for him could be enough.

But then he'd mentioned a family and her heart had nearly stopped. She tried to picture carrying a man's child without his affection. She shuddered, her eyes squeezing shut.

She'd still help him with his fear and tonight would be one of the memories she always treasured, but her future needed the sort of love that bound two people together absolutely. Otherwise…she tried to think of the alternative. The truth was she cared for him too much to suffer his indifference again. Or to watch him ride away for his own pursuits, like he'd done yesterday.

He lifted up on his arms, sliding his body forward and then he pressed down again giving her a gentle kiss. The touch was so tender, she nearly forgot her fear, her worries. Part of her longed to wrap her arms around his neck and agree to all his plans.

When he lifted up again, he pulled her night rail back down over her torso. "We should get you to bed. It's late."

A muscle in her cheek twitched. She'd only worry the more for being alone. Turning her face away, she covered her eyes with a hand. "Must I go back upstairs? My bed will be…" Lonely. But she didn't add that word. If she walked away from this man the bed was going to feel lonely for a long time.

He pressed down on top of her again. "Cold?"

That was a perfectly good word for it and she nodded. "Yes."

"If we're quiet, I can help you warm the bed before I go," he said close to her ear as he stroked her hair from her face.

"That would be nice." She coiled her arms about his neck.

Without another word, he lifted them both from the settee, carrying her from the library. Creeping through the house, they made it to her room where he set her on the cold floor. A shiver ran up her spine as she carefully opened the door. They tiptoed in and then he closed it again, sweeping her back into his arms. She'd left the covers peeled back and he quickly settled her into the bed, tucking the blankets about her body.

A moment of disappointment filled her. She'd wanted to feel him against her again. These memories would have to last a lifetime.

But he didn't leave. Instead, he sat on the bed and began removing his boots.

Her insides tugged. There was something so intimate about watching the act of him removing his shoes. She leaned up on one elbow, as the muscles in his arms flexed while he worked. "You left your shirt in the library."

He grinned back at her. "A hazard of nighttime trysts. I'll collect it before I return to my room."

She gave a small jerk of her chin as she nibbled her lip. "I wanted to say thank you," she started, scooting forward. Her eyes widened as she realized she'd been about to thank him for this great adventure. Perhaps she'd gotten her adventure after all.

"For what?" he asked, finishing with his boots and sliding under the covers, fitting her body to his.

She sighed as she snuggled into his warmth. "For this great adventure. The funny thing about reading stories is that you're always sure they will end happily. What I didn't realize about real adventures is that you're less certain of how they will end."

He held her in his arms. "That is very true. But in this case, you needn't worry. Our adventure has a happy ending."

She looked up at him, her throat tightening. "Do you really think so? I think we want different things."

He kissed the tip of her nose. "Do you want this? Snuggling in bed together?"

That was easy, her heartbeat quickened. "Yes."

"Marriage? Family? Candlelit nights by the ocean?"

"Yes to all of that."

"Then, as far as I can tell, we want the same things." He lay his head down, pressing hers into his shoulder.

She drew in a deep breath. Ophelia supposed all of that was true. "You're right. Perhaps we do want the same things but the why of it is where we differ. Why do you want me?"

He began to rhythmically stroke her back and she relaxed a bit. "I've already told you. You're perfect for me."

His words did make a girl feel good, she had to admit. A heaviness was settling over her limbs, his touch and his words soothing away her fears. "That's lovely."

"What is it you want?" he asked, peppering little kisses along her hairline.

She sighed, closing her eyes. "Well, besides everything we've already mentioned, I wanted to find a great love. Your offer is so tempting, Chase, but I'd imagined a man who loved me with all his heart." She opened her eyes to meet his. "I know I'm a fanciful dreamer. I understand that but I still wished for a man who thought I was his great love. Once I say yes to you, I've given up on that dream forever."

Words clogged his throat as Ophelia cuddled into his side. How could she not understand that he did love her? But then he realized he'd never said the words.

His mind argued back that his affection was in every caress, the way he held her now. But just this morning, he'd gotten on his horse and left her. And she was so new to physical relationships…Ophelia wasn't likely to know the difference in a man's touch when he cared for a woman versus when he did not.

Her limbs relaxed into his body, her arm across his chest and one leg over his thigh. His own lids were growing heavy, but he didn't want to be found here in the morning. That wasn't how they'd start their life together. If it was love she wanted, then he'd have to find a way to show it to her.

His mind searched for a plan until he found himself drifting off to sleep. Slowly, he slipped from the bed, hating to leave her side. He consoled himself with the knowledge they'd share a bed soon enough as husband and wife. Forever.

After grabbing his boots in his hand, he made his way out of her room and down the hall. Creeping down the stairs, he entered the library and grabbed his shirt, shrugging the garment over his head.

"I often leave my shirt in the library as well." A stone-cold male voice called from the far end of the room next to the fire.

Chase's stomach dropped as he slowly turned about. By the dim light of the fire he could just see Mr. Moorish sitting back in his desk chair. Chase straightened, not bothering to waste either of their time with denials or quibbling. "I've already asked her to marry me."

The older man rubbed his forehead. "Ophelia?"

"Yes." he set down his boots. "Who else?"

Mr. Moorish shook his head. "Best to make certain in these circumstances. Did you compromise her?"

He winced, hoping to get away with a half-truth. "I assure you her maidenhead is still intact."

"That's good at least." The man rose from his behind his desk, coming around to the front. "And I'm glad that you already proposed. I'd hate to have to force a duke, but Ophelia is the backbone of this family. I can't have her ruined—I don't mean socially, I mean emotionally."

Chase shifted on his feet. "I love your daughter." The knot in his stomach eased. Why was that so easy to say when she wasn't in front of him? "And I apologize if I've disrespected your family. I…" He held his fist. "Ophelia craves a romantic adventure and I want to give that to her to win her heart." Suddenly, all the answers became clear. If he wanted Ophelia to say yes, he had to sweep her off her feet.

The older man leaned back on his desk rubbing his face. "You're not wrong there and that's my fault. Without their mother, I've shut the girls off from the world. I didn't have much choice, I suppose. I have to work to support my family, but my daughters need to find husbands and Seabridge Gate won't provide those."

Chase shrugged. "It provided me," he answered. "Speaking of…I'll need to buy a property nearby. I can't picture Ophelia being far from her family. Do you know of any suitable ones or will I have to build?"

Mr. Moorish chuckled lightly. "Any anger I might have been harboring just disappeared. I'm sure we can find something for you. Now tell me, Your Grace, you've asked her to marry you, created a plan to woo her. I take it that she has yet to agree?"

"You're right on that front." Chase took a step back and then sat down on the very settee he and Ophelia had occupied earlier. "But I am doing my best to convince her."

"I'll intercede on your behalf. She doesn't have a choice at this point."

Chase held up a hand. "Please give me one more day. Ophelia needs this one chance to live her fairy tale."

Her father gave a stiff nod. "I can't say that I like it but if I have your assurance this will end in a marriage that includes you living near Seabridge Gate then I will consent."

Chase gave a terse nod. He'd better make this good. He needed to give Ophelia the fairy tale she craved so as to convince her to accept his proposal.

CHAPTER THIRTEEN

Ophelia woke the next day, stretching in her bed. She couldn't remember the last time she'd slept so soundly.

Then she bolted upright as memories flooded her mind. She'd allowed him to…and he'd tucked her in bed…and…

Her face flamed with heat and honestly her most intimate parts throbbed with desire. What they had done had been wicked and wonderful. She got out of bed, spinning in a small circle. If this was wooing, she liked it.

Then she covered her mouth. Chase was a rake—or had been. The heroes of her stories had been gentlemen. She'd been searching for her own fictional story come to life but perhaps reality was better. No, he hadn't declared his undying love but he had begged for her hand, held her tenderly, and made her shake with passion. Maybe this was what real women got. She went into everything in her life with fantastical expectations. Perhaps it was time to face the real world.

With that in mind, she carefully dressed, pinning her hair in an elaborate arrangement before she went down to breakfast. The day was already warming and she hummed as she made her way down the hall.

Her sisters were all talking in the breakfast room and she smiled, wondering what life would be like when she didn't hear them every day.

Stepping into the breakfast room, all conversation stopped as everyone turned to look at her. Her father sat at the head of the table, carefully sipping his tea. He didn't meet her eyes after he set down his cup. "Good morning."

Ophelia squinted, wondering about her father's chilly demeanor. "Good morning."

Bianca rested her chin on her fist. "So…" She pressed her lips together. "Anything interesting to report?"

What was happening? "No." she stepped into the room and crossed to the buffet that had been laid out already. "Not since we spoke last night."

"Really?" Juliet asked. "Nothing?"

Cordelia cleared her throat. "Come now. Ask her outright if you want to know."

"I told you girls," her father interrupted. "We're not asking her anything."

She looked over her shoulder, assessing her father's unusually drawn face. "What's the matter, Papa?"

"Nothing," he answered, rising. "We've a dinner date tonight. I'm off to work early so that I might return early." Then he walked from the room without kissing any of them goodbye.

"What's gotten into him?" She turned back to the table, making her way to her seat.

Adrianna stood, letting out a huff. "What's gotten into you? You're getting marr—"

"Adrianna, hush," Juliet bit out.

But Ophelia stopped, her plate slipping from her hand and smashing to the floor. "Don't hush. What did you just say?"

Adrianna crossed her arms, giving Juliet a black look.

Juliet stood as well. "Papa told us not to say anything. Adrianna, however, can't make it five seconds without spilling the beans."

Adrianna smacked her hand on the table. "What I don't understand is why our sister marrying a duke needs to be a secret at all."

The blood had surely drained from Ophelia's face and swayed on her feet. "Marrying a duke?"

That made all her sisters stop to look at her. "Ophelia?" Cordelia came toward her. "Are you all right?"

"What did Papa say exactly?" She pressed her hands to her cheeks trying to make her mind work. Chase had gone behind her back and asked for her father's hand when she'd yet to agree. She'd wanted a bit of romance and he'd taken even that away from her.

"That you were marrying the duke. They'd decided last night but that we shouldn't bring it up just yet." Bianca said, twisting her hands together.

Why had Papa trusted them with that information? They couldn't keep a secret to save their lives.

"I was considering his proposal but I hadn't decided yet. I know you all feel this too, but without a season, this is my one chance for flirting and romance. Papa and the duke couldn't allow me to even have one day of fun before they went behind my back to make plans." Tears came to her eyes. "I've been the grown-up since I turned sixteen. Couldn't I have just a few frivolous days?" And then she spun on her heel and left the dining room. She was angry at her father for making this choice without asking, mad at her sisters for ruining the secret, and furious with Chase for going behind her back.

She'd thought she'd been unrealistic but perhaps she hadn't been so after all. He just wasn't the man who understood her needs and how to meet them.

And she deserved better.

Chase walked down the hall, squelching the unsettling feeling that something was amiss. Despite the size of the home, which was large, he'd already grown accustomed to hearing women wherever he went in the house.

They giggled, they argued, they played music, and they danced throughout the day and into the night. But this morning the house held an eerie sort of quiet that he didn't like at all. He stopped. He and Ophelia would have to have a gaggle of children. Years of living alone had made him hungry for the sort of noise a family made.

He turned into the music room, hoping to find Ophelia. He hadn't seen her yet this morning and after all that had transpired last night, he wanted to talk with her, touch her cheek, and feel her velvety skin under his fingertips.

As he entered the room, he immediately knew something was very wrong. Ophelia wasn't there but her sisters sat silently inside. Bianca had her hands folded in her lap while Cordelia sat on the bench of the pianoforte without touching the keys.

Adrianna paced back and forth, her head shaking as her blonde hair swished over the back. Juliet stared out the window, her hand resting on the frame.

"Is something amiss?" he asked the room at large, not bothering with the niceties. They wouldn't be able to attend them anyway.

Juliet's head snapped about to look at him and she lifted her skirts, half running across the room toward him. "It's Ophelia."

Fear seized his muscles and he straightened, ready to spring into action. "What's happened. Is she hurt?"

Juliet pulled the one hand she'd fisted into her skirts and waved it in the air. "No. Nothing like that. She's just… well she's…" Juliet stopped walking and talking as she glanced up at the ceiling as though searching for the words.

His skin crawled with nervous anticipation.

"She's miserable," Adrianna filled in, taking a few steps toward him. "And you are to blame."

He rocked back on his heels. "What?"

Bianca rose from her seat, wringing her hands. "We are to blame as much as he is. We've asked so much of her and she never wishes for anything in return."

Adrianna pivoted toward her sister. "You've got me there."

Cordelia rose from the bench. "I still don't understand why father told us that His Grace and Ophelia would marry if Ophelia had yet to consent."

Adrianna fluttered her hand. "He's terrible at secrets. We all are. Me in particular."

Pricks of heat dotted his cheeks. Hell and damnation, was he blushing? He hadn't done so in years, not since he was a boy. But explaining to four innocent women all the indecent deeds he'd performed on their sister…

Juliet waved a hand toward him once again. Well, flapped might have been the better word, he thought, as a hand came decidedly close to his face. "Isn't it obvious? Papa discovered that he'd compromised our sister."

He swallowed, shifting on his feet. "I…"

"Oh." Bianca covered her cheeks. "Papa found out about the kiss."

"But how?" Cordelia asked, then pointed toward her sisters. "Which one of you told him?"

The room fell blessedly silent. He closed his eyes. He couldn't allow them to blame themselves. "He caught us, or rather me, leaving the library last night but he knew Ophelia had been there too."

"See," Adrianna said, lifting her chin higher. "It is his fault."

"But he promised me time to properly woo Ophelia. She needs the excitement of being courted that Seabridge Gate has never provided," Chase said. "I thought your father and I had agreed to give that to her."

"How sweet," Bianca sighed, her hands dropping from her face.

Juliet cleared her throat. "Oh dear. Papa did say that we should leave the two of you be because you had a marriage to work out." Juliet looked at Cordelia who had lowered her head.

"We got rather excited at the word marriage." Bianca stepped forward, taking Juliet's hand. "So it's partly our fault after all."

"What can we do?" Adrianna asked. "Ophelia deserves wooing and we just ruined it."

"I ruined it too," he volunteered. He'd been so focused on quickly convincing her to marry him that he'd trapped her in a corner. "I'm not sure I can make it up now, but I'd like to try."

"We can help," Juliet straightened. "Tell us what you need."

Well," he raised a brow. "For starters, I am going to need a lot of candles."

CHAPTER FOURTEEN

Ophelia lay in her bed, staring at the wall to her right. She'd cried out her tears some hours before and had honestly begun to feel silly for being so emotional. She'd stayed in her room because she didn't want to face her sisters.

She needed to apologize. She'd surely hurt their feelings by declaring that caring for them had been some sort of burden. She'd mostly loved it. And then, she'd had a crying fit about an engagement to a duke. Silliness.

After releasing a long sigh, she rose from the bed to walk to a bowl of water on the wash stand. Giving her face a good scrub, she gazed at her reflection, noting her still-puffy eyes and her slightly red nose. "You've gone and made a mess of this one, Ophelia," she chastised her reflection. "Papa's angry, your sisters are hurt, your fiancé thinks you don't want to marry him, all because you're holding onto a romantic fantasy of adventure and excitement." She smoothed her skirts. "It's time to start making amends and remember that you live in the real world."

But her thoughts were interrupted by the faintest tap on her windowpane. She stood straighter, cocking her head to the side as she heard the sound come again. After slowly crossing the room, she parted the curtain just enough to look out. A pebble tinkled off the glass just as she bent down. She pulled away, dropping the curtain from her hand. What the devil? Just as quickly, she bent back down again, slashing the curtain back to peer down into the growing darkness of twilight.

Below her window, Chase stood with a pile of pebbles next to him as he made ready to launch another. Her breath caught in her throat. What was going on?

Quick as she could, she unlocked the sash and raised the window. Unfortunately, Chase chose that moment to launch another small stone and it sailed through the now-open glass, glancing off her stomach. "Ouch," she said, grasping the spot. "Hold your fire."

"Oh, Ophelia," he grimaced. "Did I hit you?"

She lifted her eyebrows. "It doesn't matter. It's just a little rock. I'm more curious about why you're throwing them."

He stood taller, tucking one hand behind his back and another to his front. "I will answer your question in just a moment. First, I need to ask you one. Do you prefer the balcony scene of *Romeo and Juliet* or the first half of *Rapunzel*?"

She covered her mouth with her hand. Was he recreating a story for her? New fresh tears sprang to her eyes, but these were of joy, not sorrow. Still she quickly blinked them away. "*Rapunzel*. She actually gets to be with her prince."

He gave a nod, a smile spreading across his lips. "I was hoping you'd say that." Clearing his throat, he called up. "Rapunzel, Rapunzel—"

She held up a finger. "Are you going to climb up my hair? Because I think that might hurt and I'm not sure it's long enough to reach down three stories."

He quirked a brow. "Who loves fairy tales here? Where is your imagination?"

"Funny you should ask because I've been thinking that I should—"

"Hang on," he called up. "I'll be right there."

Her lips parted as she watched him dash to the door near the kitchen. Closing the window, she stood in the middle of the room wondering what she was supposed to do.

She didn't have to wait long. She heard his footfalls in the hall and then her door swung open. "I'm not a prince but…" He paused with a smile.

She grinned back. "I think a duke will do."

He held out his hand. "If you'll permit me, my lady, I'd like to sweep you away on our own private rendezvous."

Her breath caught. Where would they go? What would they do? Excitement beat in her chest as she finally understood what his plan was. "Yes," she whispered and then louder. "Oh yes."

Without waiting for her to take his hand, he crossed the room and swept her into his arms. "Right this way, my love. Time for your own love story."

CHASE SWEPT Ophelia into his arms, hoping the gesture made up for the gaffes. He'd hit her with a rock, he'd left her standing as he'd raced up the stairs. He'd fashioned a rope ladder, actually, to get her down. Her father had loads of rope out in the barn but the way things were going, he hadn't wanted to risk it.

She let out a little yelp but a smile graced her lips and her eyes crinkled in merriment. "Where are we going?"

He turned them sideways to fit out the door. "Shhhh. I hear your father will be home soon and I don't want him to discover that I've carried you away."

Her nose twitched. "He'll notice when I don't attend dinner."

"The jackals are coming. They'll distract him."

"Jackals?" They made it down the stairs and started for the door.

"Lord Crestwood and his crew of delinquents," he said, starting for the path that led down to the ocean. He'd spent the day by the water to prepare for their romantic rendezvous. To his surprise, he'd enjoyed the seaside far more than he'd ever imagined. First, the sisters had shown him a little cover carved out of the rocks, hidden from view and protected by wind. The sand was dry as a bone and Juliet had assured him the water never washed into that section.

He'd laid out blankets, set up candles, and brought down a basket of food. The sisters had helped him, chattering in their way. For the first time in his adult life the ocean signified a joining of family rather than a parting. And he'd been forced to admit, as long as he didn't have to go in the water, watching the waves had a certain charm.

She tapped his shoulder. "Do you think we should be there? My sisters are so innocent and—"

"More innocent than you?" He leaned down and kissed her lips as he stared down the steep rocky path.

She kissed him back, her tongue meeting his in a searing kiss. "Definitely."

When he pulled back from her lips, he rubbed his nose against hers. "I warned them that Lord Crestwood and his friends were rakes of the first order. It's time for your sisters to take care of themselves. Just a bit."

She parted her mouth to argue and he silenced her with another kiss. "I warned your father too. He'll keep them safe enough."

"How did you warn my father without revealing that you were sweeping me away to the beach?"

He chuckled. "I told him that I had to go fetch a ring." They reached the shoreline and he started for the little alcove in the rocks. "It was a bit of a white lie. One I hope he'll forgive me for."

"You have a ring already or you have no intention of buying one?" she asked as he gently set her on her feet.

"Cover your eyes," he whispered close to her ear.

"And to answer your question, both. I have a ring already so I've no need to buy one." He was slowly leading her toward the cove, her feet shuffling as she covered her eyes. Normally he would have carried her but he had another surprise in mind and he needed her to be standing.

Finally, he stopped just in the entrance of the cove. He was pleased to see that most of the candles had remained lit and his blankets were still spread about the sand.

"What do you need a ring for?" she asked, but he knew she understood, her fingers had begun shaking in his.

"Just give me one more moment, my love, and I will explain everything." And then he dropped down on one knee.

CHAPTER FIFTEEN

Ophelia shifted in the sand, anticipation making it difficult to stay still. "Can I open my eyes yet?"

"Almost."

His deep, rich voice made her shiver in excitement. This moment, right here, was everything she'd ever wanted. A handsome man had swept her away to an unknown surprise. She pressed her free hand to her cheek. "Now?"

"Now," he answered.

She opened her eyes and the first thing she noticed was the soft glow of light coming from the alcove in the rocks. She and her sisters had played here often as children and she'd spent many an afternoon curled in the sand with a beloved book. Now the hollowed-out rock formation was lit with… "There must be fifty candles."

"One hundred," Chase said softly.

His voice made her breath catch but she couldn't look away from the scene. Blankets and pillows had been spread about in the shelter and a basket sat to one side. "Is it a picnic?"

"Yes." He laced his fingers through hers.

"I've never been to a candlelight picnic before. In some ways it looks more like the fantasy I described…" Her words tapered off as she turned to look at him and realized he had dropped to one knee.

And he was holding out a box in one hand.

And he was smiling in a certain way…as though they had a special secret no one else shared.

"It does. Doesn't it?" Then he let go of her hand and cracked open the tiny, intricately carved wooden box. In it lay delicately folded satin and a gold ring with a large sapphire in its center.

She gasped as he removed the ring from the folds and reached for her hand again. "Miss Ophelia Moorish, would you do me the honor of becoming my wife?"

Her lip trembled as he waited for her answer. "I should tell you something before I answer."

His brow crinkled and he leaned back a bit. "What?"

She swallowed. "It's just that…well I find that…I

am in love with you." She drew in a breath. "And I know that you don't feel that way about me, but I want you to know before we go any further that I'd like those feelings to grow between us. If you don't think that can happen then I'm not certain I should say yes."

He stood, his eyes crinkling at the corners as he pulled her closer. "It can't happen in the future."

"Oh." Her heart sunk to her knees and she blinked several times because she refused to cry any more today. "I understand."

"You don't." And then he pulled her left hand toward him, slipping the ring on her finger. "I can't fall in love with you in the future because I am in love with you now. I wanted to deny it but I think you might have stolen my heart from the first moment we met." Then he pulled her close and kissed her. Her chest swelled with emotion even as her body hummed with desire. This…this was exactly the fairy tale she'd always wished to have. Only it was even better because this fairy tale was real.

OPHELIA TREMBLED IN HIS ARMS, meeting each of

Chase's kisses with a passion that stole the breath from his lungs.

She twined her fingers into his hair as her mouth parted under his, their tongues tangling together. He lifted her again, carrying her into the alcove, where they were sheltered and warmed by the candles. Laying her down on the blankets, he pulled another over them, creating a cozy sanctuary.

She pulled away and gave him a grin. "Am I going to have to give you the ring back so you can propose again at a sanctioned meeting?"

His eyes widened and he chuckled. "I suppose so, although, I hate to see the jewel removed from your hand. It looks so perfect on you." He reached for her fingers, bringing them to his lips. "The ring was my mother's favorite."

She gasped and looked at the stone again. "You had this with you?"

He shrugged. "I carry a cravat of my father's as well. To be honest, putting the ring on your hand…I feel like she's part of our future." He leaned his forehead down to touch hers. "I've been searching for my future for a long time, growing increasingly restless and now…I am at peace."

She grasped his face. "I am too." Then she kissed him again, hard and long. "Chase." There was an edge to her voice that made his heart race in his chest. "I want to live out the whole fantasy tonight. I want to make love to you under the stars."

He growled out his need, trying to calm his body's driving need. "Ophelia, we should wait until we're married."

She shook her head. "This is our night. We begin our future together here and now." She slid her fingers down his neck and into the V of his open shirt.

His pulse raced as she touched him. "Ophelia. Do you have any idea how desirable you are? Good God, woman, you could drive a man to…" He looked down at her, searching for the word.

"Remain faithful?" She quirked a brow.

He grimaced. "You needn't worry, my love. I was searching for you and now that search is over." He kissed her again, trying to express the depths of his emotion in a single kiss. But the kiss wasn't enough. He pulled up, shrugging his shirt over his head. Then he leaned back down and brought Ophelia to him before working on the row of buttons at the back of her dress.

Her bodice slumped forward and she lay down again, wriggling the fabric over her hips. In response, he started working the ties of her corset, saying a silent prayer she wore short stays. In a flurry of activity, they stripped down several more layers, both frantic to touch each other's skin.

He caressed her everywhere. Cruising his hands over her torso, down her arms, across her thighs, around her back. He touched her as though he created a map. The swell of her hips, like rolling hills, her stomach a valley. And when he brushed through the curls between her legs, they both groaned.

She traced the ridges of his back and then slid her hands into his trousers, touching his backside. "Take down your pants, I want to see all of you."

He wanted to see her too. But Chase worried just a bit. Passionate as she was, Ophelia was still a virgin and the male sex could be rather…intimidating. "Are you certain you're ready for it? We can just do what we did last time."

She shook her head, reaching up to his face and grazing her thumb over his lip. "No. This is our big moment and I will not squander our opportunity because I got scared. Heroes and heroines take the big risks."

He had to smile. "It's not huge. Perhaps just right."

"Are we discussing the risk or something else?"

He started pulling her shift up over her hips. "The danger, mostly. There is no chance I am letting you get away from me. You will be my wife very soon."

She sighed and lifted to allow him to pull the garment over her head. "That's just perfect."

CHAPTER SIXTEEN

She tried to imagine a better scenario. This…this was even more wonderful than their first kiss in the library had been. She scooted down her pantaloons and stockings until she lay naked under the blanket. Chase stood and removed his boots, then pulled off his breeches.

She shivered as she studied him. Not huge? Ophelia propped herself up on one elbow. Having full access to the library and being an avid reader, she'd done her fair share of studying the medical journals. She understood the basics of copulation but none of the diagrams she'd seen had even come close to looking like the member currently jutting out from his body. "That is going inside me?"

One corner of his mouth ticked up. "Believe it or

not, women are rather fond of a larger…" He looked down.

She shook her head, fear making her jaw clench. "Good to know."

He lay down next to her, pulling the blanket back over himself and fitting his body against hers. His skin was slightly cool but immediately began to warm. "My offer still stands. We can save making love for our wedding night."

She drew in a deep breath, forcing herself to relax. "No, I'm ready now. I won't be a coward in the face of my fear or yours."

"My fear?" he asked, kissing the sensitive spot on her neck.

She ran her hand over his muscled chest. "I know how you feel about the ocean. Today I want to give you a new memory. I can't change what happened in the past, but I want to help balance out your feelings involving the water. It gives and takes away."

He pushed up on his arms as she rolled onto her back. "Have you ever considered yourself the hero in your stories rather than the heroine?"

She stilled, her lips parting. "Well. That is interesting. I suppose I like that idea very much."

"I'm glad because you, my love, have saved me." Then he pressed down and captured her lips again.

There were no more words as they kissed,

lengthening and deepening, their bodies pressed together.

Every inch of his muscled frame heated hers as her legs twined with his. Then he kissed lower, along her neck, chest, and down to her nipples. She cried out when he sucked one into his mouth, her heart beating in rhythm to his.

And when his fingers brushed through her folds, pleasure tightened her skin.

"You feel so wonderful," he murmured against her chest. "Like a dream."

"Or a fairy tale." She smiled until he inserted a finger into her channel.

He moved to the other nipple. Using another finger in her body. This one stretched her open further and while the pleasure was still there, it burned just a bit. "You're so tight."

"See. Now you know why I was concerned." She gasped out as he spread her a bit wider.

He slid back up, giving her a slow kiss on the lips. "Ophelia...we don't—"

"I want you inside me," she whispered looking into his eyes.

Chase stopped, his face tightening as his gaze darkened. He slipped his fingers out as his hips settled over hers, his member pressing to her opening. Though a bit scary, the tip also rubbed her in such a way as to make shivers of pleasure shoot through her legs. "Oh," she moaned, moving her hips to feel more. And then he sank inside her, just a bit, spreading her open. "I see what you mean," she said between breaths. "It pulls a bit but also, something about the shape, you can tell it was made to be inside me. Even now, it feels good."

He buried his face into the crook of her neck. "Ophelia, I swear on all that is holy, that you're going to undo me. I love that you talk so much during the most intimate times, my love, but I am trying to maintain control so that I don't hurt you and you telling me how good I feel, how I'm made to be inside you. I swear, it's driving me mad."

She knew those words were a warning but she wasn't sure she cared to hear it. She loved this intimacy between them and his desire for her was worth a bit of pain. It made her feel powerful, attractive, and wanted. "Would it also drive you mad to know that I love the hair on your body? It's rough and masculine. The way your muscles are sculpted makes me want to lick you from…" He pushed all the way inside her, breaking her maidenhead in one quick push. They both stilled. "Oh. That did hurt."

He smoothed her hair back from her face. "Tell me about your next romantic fantasy. Would we be on an island?"

WHEN ONLY AN INDECENT DUKE WILL DO

She shook her head. "That would require a boat."

"You are so wonderful. Do you know that?" And he kissed her hard.

"Well," she started. "We still haven't used the rose petals. Perhaps we'll spread those on our bed. Oh. Can it be a large four post with curtains?"

He slowly pulled out of her and gently pushed back in, it hardly hurt at all. "Of course. But I'd request that we repeat the candles. I love all this light."

She liked it too. She wanted to explore every inch of him. "Oh yes, and..." She paused as he moved into her again, but this time it didn't hurt nearly as much. "When we were young, we'd tickle each other with ostrich feathers. Do you think they'd be a nice touch?"

His entire body spasmed. "Ophelia," he growled as he thrust into her again. The pain was gone and in its place was the most amazing sort of pleasure that even her toes curled. She dug her fingers into the small of his back, whimpering and pressing their hips closer together.

"So, I'm going to lay you down in a bed of rose petals and run feathers all over your body. What else?"

Pleasure was spiraling through her and she squeezed her eyes shut as her body tightened around his. "I don't know but I'm sure you'll teach me."

He pressed into her again. "You're right. We've got all the time in the world to learn." Holding onto her tighter, he increased the rhythm as their bodies moved as one. Soon, she couldn't hold back and her pleasure crashed around her like a wave breaking on the shore.

She cried out just as his own finish overtook him, his body shaking in release.

As he collapsed on top of her, Ophelia closed her eyes and sighed with pleasure. This was her happily ever after after all.

EPILOGUE

Two months later...

Ophelia stood near the top of the bluffs, the summer sun shining down as her sisters fanned out beside her. A soft breeze ruffled her silk gown as Chase held both her hands. Next to him stood his cousin, the Marquess of Hartwell. He'd made the journey for the wedding, and Ophelia was so grateful that Chase had family with him today.

The local vicar stood in front of them, giving them each a smile.

"It is with great pleasure that I wed Ophelia Moorish to His Grace here at Seabridge Gate."

As the ceremony began the words washed over her, her hand joined to Chase's. They'd chosen only to have their family here and of course, Lord Crestwood, Lord Craven, and Lord Dashlane. Because the party was so small, they'd agreed to have their wedding breakfast in the alcove on the beach. Together, they'd make new memories.

"I now pronounce you man and wife," Vicar Williams announced. "You may kiss the bride."

The crowd cheered, her father loudest of all, as Chase softly kissed her lips, drawing her close to him. "This is our future, my love."

She sighed, loving those words on his lips. "I'd like to think that this is our present and our future holds even better things." It had taken close to two months to get her father to agree to a short engagement and for his cousin to arrive. And while she couldn't be certain, they'd managed to sneak away at regular intervals, leaving her with the suspicion she was carrying his child. She hadn't bled in weeks.

He quirked a brow as he threaded her hand into his elbow and led the procession down the bluff to their prepared picnic. "What could be better than this?"

She shrugged, giving him a soft smile. She didn't want to share yet, just in case she was wrong, but soon enough she'd be able to tell him that they were building a family of their own. And that was a dream come true for both of them. "Well for starters, I'll be able to stay in your bed tonight."

He grinned, giving her a wink. "That is very true," he leaned down to whisper in her ear. "I can't wait to sleep the entire night with you tucked by my side."

She giggled back. "Is that all we'll do, Your Grace?"

He gave her a sly grin but didn't answer as they made it to the beach.

For the next two hours, they ate and chatted with their family and friends, spread out on blankets in the shade of the rocks before Chase pulled her to her feet again. "It's time," he said, waving to everyone else.

"Time for what?" she asked.

"Time for you to see your new home," her father inserted, looking absolutely delighted. "Are you surprised?"

What were they talking about? "New home?"

Chase took both her hands. "I've purchased a property here at Seabridge Gate. The house is small but it will be perfect for now while we build a grander one."

Tears filled her eyes. "You bought a house. Here?"

He gave a wide grin. "This will be our home. We're rewriting those memories of the sea, remember?" Then he leaned even closer. "And I've got a few more surprises for you too."

She could barely contain herself as they made their way to the top of the bluff and climbed into a waiting carriage. It only took fifteen minutes to make their way to the other side of Seabridge Gate. The carriage stopped in front of the old Chesterfield Farm. Rolling hills spread out from the sea and a small colonial sat at the end of the drive. "I've always loved this property."

He squeezed her hand as he helped her out of the carriage. "Come inside."

They breezed past the small staff that waited for them with a short hello and then headed up the stairs. At the end of the hall, he opened the double doors. Inside the room, stood a large, four post bed sprinkled with dozens of pale pink rose petals.

"Chase." She covered her mouth but then dropped her hands. "Did you get the feathers?"

He laughed as he lifted her and swung her about in a circle. "What my lady asks for, she receives. Now and always."

Sighing, she kissed his lips as her toes brushed the ground. "I'm so glad I managed to find such an indecent husband," she murmured against his lips. "This shall be fun indeed."

UNTITLED

How to Catch an Elusive Earl
  Romancing the Rake Book 2

Tammy Andresen

CHAPTER SEVENTEEN

Lucius Marks, the Earl of Crestwood, assessed the

stately manor as the last rays of sun set in the sky. *How nauseatingly pretty*, Luke thought as the bright rays bathed the red brick in bright hues of orange and yellow. Below him, the ocean beat against the high rocks of the bluff, creating a scene fit for a work of art.

This house was like the rest of Seabridge Gate, the village he currently found himself stranded in: disgustingly wholesome.

He sighed, regretting his decision to come to this dinner, and he hadn't even gone inside yet. Which was ridiculous. This entire affair had been his idea to begin with. In his defense, the meal with the Moorish family was a sound plan. First because he needed Mr. Moorish's help. The man ran a shipping business out of Seabridge Gate and catching a ride on one of those ships was his best chance of getting out of this quaint little hell hole and making his way north to a deliciously debaucherous gathering being held by the Baron of Balstead.

Just thinking of that party and all the delights that would surely greet him made his spine straighten with determination. The bridge to the north had washed out, making the trip to Balstead's property in Haversham days longer than was necessary. Meanwhile, if he could catch a boat, say tomorrow morning, he'd be at Balstead's by lunch. And wrapped in a woman's arms by dinner.

And so he raised the knocker on the door, letting it fall from his hand. Luke heard the sound echo through the house. The door immediately opened, a sharp-looking butler giving him a solemn stare. "Good evening. Lord Crestwood, I presume?"

"Correct," he answered. "I've clearly arrived at the right place."

The man gestured for him to step inside. "Are Lord Craven and Lord Dashlane joining you?"

He gave a momentary grimace before replacing the look with a firm smile. Yesterday, his friends, Craven and Dashlane, had met the eldest Moorish daughter, Miss Ophelia Moorish. He couldn't be entirely certain, but he suspected that she might have infected them with a dose of morality. She'd been incredibly beautiful but also so kind that a man might get ideas about the sort of life he should be living. "No, they've other business to attend in the village."

Not him, of course. Luke had been firmly and completely expunged of any wholesome hope several years ago. A woman who seemed to be the very pinnacle of goodness and light had so thoroughly broken his heart that he'd devowed ever taking such a risk again.

Which was why he planned to not only secure passage on one of Moorish's ships, he also intended to steal a kiss or two from one of the other four Moorish daughters. He pulled his lips down to keep from giving a salacious grin. If he were going to be stuck in such a place, he may as well leave a little mark upon it. It was the duty of all rakes to do so.

"Very good, then. Right this way, my lord." The butler turned and started up the stairs, Luke following.

Reaching the second floor, they made their way down the hall where the butler stopped in the doorway. "May I present his lordship, the Earl of Crestwood."

Luke held back his grunt of disdain. He was as fond of the title as he was of wholesome pursuits. None of them were meant to be his.

The Honorable Thomas Moorish rose along with four young women, each a delight in her own way. He swept his gaze down the line of them, attempting to decide which might be his favorite. Moorish gave him a welcoming smile. "Good evening, my lord. So nice to see you again."

"And you," he gave a nod, his gaze drifting to the man's daughters again.

"Right," Moorish pointed to the first of the ladies

in the line. "My daughter, Miss Juliet. I believe the two of you met yesterday."

They had. She was a darling little auburn-haired confection with curves like Ophelia's but a more trusting nature. She'd do nicely for his purposes.

"And this is Cordelia," Lord Moorish pointed to a serious looking, but very pretty woman that Luke dismissed on the spot. She'd never fall for a rake's charm. Even now, as she stared back at him, her eyes sparkled with intelligence.

"My daughter, Bianca." Mr. Moorish pointed to the third woman in the line.

Bianca gave a bit of a giggle and a wave and he returned a smile. She was a contender for certain. He stood straighter wondering which delightful miss he'd like to taste.

Lord Moorish pointed to the last girl down the line. "And this is Adrianna."

Luke glanced at the last woman, dismissing her from the first. She was slender for starters, more so than any of her sisters, and he liked some good curves to hold onto. While her features might have been the most perfectly symmetrical and beautiful he'd ever seen, there was a hardness about her eyes that told him she'd not be interested in what he had in mind. "A pleasure, ladies."

"We're very much looking forward to dining with

you, my lord, but first lets you and I discuss the schedule tomorrow." Mr. Moorish gestured toward a chair for Luke to sit. "We've a boat that will be stopping to pick up additional goods in Haversham that leaves at noon. If you're still interested in heading north, you're more than welcome to board it."

Luke slapped his thigh, his first objective already met. "Thank you, most kind of you."

Lord Moorish held up his hand. "Please understand this isn't a passenger ship. We keep a tight schedule and if you're not on that boat by eleven forty-five, it sails without you."

Luke gave a single nod. "I understand. Perfectly. Eleven forty-five." Silently, he gave a cheer. That left plenty of time for drinking tonight and to drag himself from bed in the morning to board that boat.

"You must have very important business in Haversham that you are working so hard to get there." Juliet straightened her skirts about her knees, her slender hands, drawing his attention to the lovely silk of her gown.

He hated the rumble of guilt that reverberated through his chest as he tried to think of an appropriate answer. Why should he feel guilty lying to these women? He didn't. Nor would he allow guilt at the idea of stealing a little peck. A kiss was almost no harm, it wasn't like he intended to leave one with child. She might even like such a romantic adventure. Experience. "Indeed. Important land deal," he muttered trying to give as little detail as possible.

"Really," Adrianna asked, leaning forward. "A land deal? Are Lord Dashlane and Lord Craven also participating in this deal?"

He looked at the last Moorish sister, attempting to quell his irritation. Her bright blues eyes stared back at him, one eyebrow slightly cocked and her chin notched at a jaunty angle that dared him to continue to lie. What a minx. His blood surged in his veins. Dare accepted.

ADRIANNA MOORISH STARED at the cad who currently lounged in her sitting room as though he were a dear member of the family and not some snake outsider come to pillage their fruits.

She drew in a breath, puffing out her small chest. Not on her watch. She might be the youngest Moorish but she was also the strongest. She'd developed a razor-sharp tongue over the years, likely because it had been her only defense in her youth against the onslaught of four older sisters who were all bigger and stronger. She was still the smallest, of course, but in all likelihood, the most feared.

Not that she'd ever truly hurt her sisters, she'd protect them with every tool she had, just as they would her. But this man had come for nefarious purposes and she was going to cut him down until he skulked away in tears. All right. She couldn't actually picture the earl crying, but he'd skulk. There would be definite skulking. There was no doubt about that.

Just as she'd make certain he didn't go near any of her sisters. She'd been given this task and she had every intention of completing the job. Her soon-to-be brother in law, the Duke of Rathmore, had pulled her aside earlier in the day and warned her that Crestwood was the worst sort of gentleman. He'd told her not to allow any of her sisters near the man and certainly not to allow them to be alone with him.

Adrianna had scrunched her brow, staring at her Rathmore. "Why are you telling me all of this?"

Rathmore had given her a pat on the shoulder. "Because you are just the Moorish to keep him in check. He's a rake, Adrianna, through and through. Don't allow his charming smile to win you over and don't let him anywhere near your sisters. Juliet and Bianca are so trusting. Please watch over them tonight."

Adrianna levelled Crestwood with another glare.

She was ready, and Rathmore was correct on both counts. This man was the worst sort of rogue, she could see it in his every gesture, and Adrianna was the woman for the job when it came to protecting her family. "Well, my lord, are you going to answer my question?"

He sat up straighter, his grin growing brittle as more of his teeth showed. He was a wolf, a handsome wolf, but a predator nonetheless. "What question was that? I've forgotten."

"What sort of land deal are you and your friends venturing into that cannot wait?" She sat straighter, a triumphant smile surely curling her lips. This was a topic she actually had some knowledge on, making it a perfect one to highlight his deceitful nature. Her sisters would surely see what a snake he was by the time she was done. She'd bet her dowry he was lying.

Adrianna might have just told her sisters outright that the man was no good but she'd seen firsthand that it wouldn't work. Juliet wouldn't believe her, and in all likelihood, her elder sister would just spend that much more time with the man, trying to prove Adrianna wrong.

Crestwood's mouth turned down further but he didn't respond as her father interceded. "Adrianna, that's not something our guest need answer."

Drat, she tapped her fan against her knee. She'd

nearly had Crestwood trapped. Any parcel of land large enough for three lords to consider buying together, had a very limited pool of buyers. Which meant there was likely no competition for the sale. So why the rush?

"I'm simply making conversation, Papa. Shouldn't I be interested in the topic our guest had mentioned for discussion?"

Her father frowned and muttered something about an interrogation, but she ignored the word.

Instead, she turned back to Crestwood and put on her best smile, trying to relax her brow in the hopes of looking kind rather than accusatory. "Isn't that right, Lord Crestwood? You mentioned the deal. Wouldn't you say it was polite to ask questions?"

He gave her a long look, turning his head first one way and then the other. "Polite isn't quite the word that came to mind."

She gave a delicate sniff, pretending not to understand his meaning. Two could play this game. "I find real estate quite fascinating. For example, did you know that the Louisiana Purchase was over two million kilometers?"

"Fascinating," he replied, sitting back in his chair. His tone implied he'd found it anything but as his arms relaxed at his side, she narrowed her gaze. He was stepping directly into her trap.

Adrianna leaned forward. "Now that is a tract of land fit for three lords of your stature."

"Quite," he answered, crossing one knee over the other as his gaze drifted to her sister Bianca. He looked like a cat about to steal the milk. His square jaw flexed even as his dark eyes glittered with nefarious interest. His arms flexed as he wrapped his large hands about his knee. For just a moment, she watched his long, tapered fingers lace together. Oh, he was handsome. That was for certain. It's part of what made him so dangerous.

Not to her, of course. No matter how masculine he looked, she was not fooled. Despite having grown up in this tiny hamlet, she considered herself smart enough to do battle with the likes of a rake. It was her best asset and the one that would keep her sisters safe as they all hunted for husbands. Bianca was a lovely woman with a heart of gold, but she'd never defend herself against a man like this. Which was why Adrianna needed to frighten him away right this minute before one of her sisters succumbed to his good looks and charm.

"Now in Haversham, there are only three parcels that could possibly suffice for such a transaction that you'd be interested in making. I'm truly curious. Which one are you considering?"

His knee dropped back down, his gaze fixing on

her as the muscles in his face hardened. "Which one?"

"Yes." she placed her most innocent smile on her face. "Which tract of land are you referring to?" It was difficult, but she kept from crowing over her victory. She had him. Haversham was part of her family's holdings. Not her father's, of course, but his older brother's, The Earl of Seabridge.

He slowly sat up in his chair, as a hand came to the back of his neck, giving the skin a careful rub. "Well," he started and his Adam's apple bobbed up and down. "The one closest to Haversham proper, of course." Then he turned to her father, his look brightening. "And if this deal works the way I hope it does, perhaps we can discuss the shipment of our newest goods. It would be a natural pairing."

Her father brightened considerably. "Now you're talking." Her father gave her a pat on the knee. "Adrianna is excessively intelligent. And here I was thinking she didn't have a point to her questions, but look where she led us. Well done, my sweet girl."

Adrianna snapped her mouth closed. She noted that Crestwood still hadn't named a specific plot or the type of product he'd need shipped. But her father was always eager to make a new deal and Crestwood must have realized that. Now her father wouldn't allow her to interrupt for certain. She'd have to find another way to expose him for the rake he was.

Irritation bristled along her skin. He was good, she'd give him that, but this fight wasn't over. Far from it. The night had just begun.

Want to read more? How to Catch an Elusive Earl is the second book in the Romance the Rake series!

Also in the Romancing the Rake series:
   Where to Woo a Bawdy Baron
   What a Vulgar Viscount Needs
   Why a Marauding Marquess is Best
   Who Wants a Brawling Baron
   When to Dare an Indecent Duke

Keep up with all the latest news, sales, freebies, and releases by joining my newsletter!

www.tammyandresen.com

Hugs!

ABOUT THE AUTHOR

Tammy Andresen lives with her husband and three children just outside of Boston, Massachusetts. She grew up on the Seacoast of Maine, where she spent countless days dreaming up stories in blueberry fields and among the scrub pines that line the coast. Her mother loved to spin a yarn and Tammy filled many hours listening to her mother retell the classics. It was inevitable that at the age of eighteen, she headed off to Simmons College, where she studied English literature and education. She never left Massachusetts but some of her heart still resides in Maine and her family visits often.

Find out more about Tammy:
http://www.tammyandresen.com/
https://www.facebook.com/authortammyandresen
https://twitter.com/TammyAndresen
https://www.pinterest.com/tammy_andresen/
https://plus.google.com/+TammyAndresen/

Read Tammy Andresen's other books:

Seeds of Love: Prequel to the Lily in Bloom series

Lily in Bloom

Midnight Magic

OTHER TITLES BY TAMMY

How to Reform a Rake

Don't Tell a Duke You Love Him

Meddle in a Marquess's Affairs

Never Trust an Errant Earl

Never Kiss an Earl at Midnight

Make a Viscount Beg

Wicked Lords of London

Earl of Sussex

My Duke's Seduction

My Duke's Deception

My Earl's Entrapment

My Duke's Desire

My Wicked Earl

Brethren of Stone

The Duke's Scottish Lass

Scottish Devil

Wicked Laird

Kilted Sin

Rogue Scot

The Fate of a Highland Rake

A Laird to Love

Christmastide with my Captain

My Enemy, My Earl

Heart of a Highlander

A Scot's Surrender

A Laird's Seduction

Taming the Duke's Heart

Taming a Duke's Reckless Heart

Taming a Duke's Wild Rose

Taming a Laird's Wild Lady

Taming a Rake into a Lord

Taming a Savage Gentleman

Taming a Rogue Earl

Fairfield Fairy Tales

Stealing a Lady's Heart

Hunting for a Lady's Heart

Entrapping a Lord's Love: Coming in February of 2018

American Historical Romance

Lily in Bloom

Midnight Magic

The Golden Rules of Love

Boxsets!!

Taming the Duke's Heart Books 1-3

American Brides

A Laird to Love

Wicked Lords of London

Printed in Great Britain
by Amazon